First

Light

First Light

A Guardian Book

DB Markham

ISBN 979-8-9910545-3-9 (Paperback preprint edition)

Library of Congress Control Number 2024925290

Printed and bound in the USA
First printing December 2024

Published by DB Markham
1800 Fescue Circle
Huddleston VA 24104

A Bad Day

*Whan I was a childe, I spake as a childe, I vnderstode as
a childe, I ymagined as a childe. But as soone as I was a
man, I put awaye childishness*

TCB, 1535

THE WORST PART OF TUESDAY WASN'T WRITHING IN PAIN, having
flames shoot from her head, voiding her bowels and dying in
screaming agony in front of a crowd of cheering onlookers. No,
the worst part of Tuesday for Beverly Castler was finding out that the
afterlife began in Newark, New Jersey. What a dump.

Warden Smithers led off the festivities with a 3 a.m. visit. She had
been told to dress to expect important visitors.

Entering her cell, Smithers saw that Beverly did not disappoint. Perfectly put-together grey hair, a business suit of dark grey and white, fine,
expensive antique jewelry, and always the razor-sharp predator blue-grey
eyes. The Murdering Madame of Manchester sat perfectly upright in her
chair in her room, moving only slightly to acknowledge him as the guard
passed Smithers through.

To others, Beverly Castler was an extremely bad person who also did
extremely good things. To herself, Beverly was an extremely good person
who also did extremely bad things. Best described by one reporter as a
"cross between Martha Stewart and Hannibal Lechter," she was sixty-two,
the oldest woman on death row, the woman serial killer with the high-
est body count, the woman two-dozen books had been written about,
and the only woman the state had given a closed trial, including sealed

records. She was also the only woman Smithers ever met that was both loved and hated by everyone she met.

It was unnerving. She affected him. Watching others interact with Beverly reminded Smithers of watching deer, trapped in oncoming headlights. She made them all interested, scared, bemused, fearful, and frozen.

Dead.

"Warden Smithers, how good to see you," She smiled warmly. She pushed forward a gift-wrapped box, "This is something for Lisa. Not much, but all I could do."

"Lisa? My wife?" he managed.

"Of course! Her birthday is coming up this week. Forty-three,right? If I'm not mistaken next week is your twenty-second anniversary as well. Best wishes to you all. Made this myself," she pointed to the small box. "I've got another gift coming next week."

"Beverly, I have another letter for you," he pulled out the envelope.

"Let's see, press, writers, TV, bloggers, victims, death row advocates, potential suitors? Personal delivery, must be special."

"It is," he opened it and got his glasses out. "It's from the mother of little Timothy Beavers, the one you flayed alive and put into the stew for customers visiting your house of prostitution."

"Oh dear," she said, "I imagine it's quite negative, dark, and dreary. Little Timothy was such a sweet boy."

Smithers didn't know how to take that. Instead, he held it up, "Should I read it?"

She stuffed it in her pocket.

"Heavens no! I get several of those a week. I don't blame those poor souls for being so unforgiving. I hope the letters help them, bless them. Don't we have more pressing business?"

"You probably won't have time later," he paused for just a second, then gave up. He slowly rose from her table, ushering her up. "Today's a big day. We've got a surprise."

"Something's wrong, I can tell, Lucas," she said, "Governor's finally visiting?"

He nodded, but slowly. She finished standing.

"And I suppose he's ready to deal, hence all these middle-of-the-night shenanigans. That man is so tiresome. Always has been."

He began walking her down the hall. He let her go first. There was no point in giving up manners, even at a time like this. She smiled as she noticed his consideration.

"I'm not so sure about that, Beverly," he managed again, the words coming rougher and rougher. He was walking beside her. He'd witnessed more than twenty executions, but nothing like tonight. "You might be wanting to make your peace with the maker."

"Oh don't be so drab, Lucas. If the Governor's here, things are looking up. Trust me."

Reaching the end of the hall, he pointed to the left.

"Why that way?" she asked, "The interview rooms are to the right."

He said nothing.

"Lucas, even if they're here to kill me, the execution chamber is also the other way." She was a kind matron indulging a minor slip-up on his part.

He could say nothing. Instead he pointed to the left again. They began walking to the door at the end of that hall. The old one.

It was an ancient metal door, part of the old prison. It hadn't been renovated with everything else 20 years back. The old chrome knob was dented, scruffy, weathered, scratched. They were visiting something of a museum piece. They were visiting something the guards would bring friends in to see. When nobody would get in trouble, when finally apprehending a killer, Law Enforcement still joked about this room. But never in public, never where they could be recorded.

A black plaque on the door. It read "Old Sparky."

"In here," he opened the door and they both went in. He closed the door behind them.

They were in a semi-circular room with windows for walls. Curtains had been drawn over the windows. The smell of old leather and dust hung deeply in the moist air.

In the middle of the room was something that looked like it might be a dentist's chair straight out of an old western. It was covered in an old black drop cloth. Smithers flipped a switch. Fluorescents flickered to life. Along one wall was a row of switches. She thought that it looked like something out of an ancient black-and-white horror film.

"Old Sparky? Seriously?" She smiled while shaking her head and tut-tutting, a schoolmarm amused at some expected but lame juvenile hijinks. "I know better than that. What kind of charade is this? Some kind of mind game? I'm scheduled for lethal injection, and that's over a week from today."

Smithers pulled the cover from the chair. Cockroaches scurried for cover from the harsh light.

"If the Governor thinks this negotiating tactic will work, he's got another thing coming."

She sounded firm, but not as firm as before, Smithers thought. He could see her body tighten as if she had just read his mind.

A cold chill ran down his spine. It wasn't the first time Beverly Castler had that effect on him, but he suspected it was the last. He hoped. Goosebumps overtook his arms and shoulders, threatened his back.

"Beverly," he said, walking over to the curtains, "I'm 53. I've been a warden for eleven years now. I've seen a lot of things."

He pulled the rope, opening the curtains up.

"But yours is the first surprise execution I've ever witnessed. May God have mercy on your soul."

She took a step back, as if attacked and preparing to defend herself.

It was the first time he'd seen The Gallery like this. The Gallery was usually a somber place. It always had extra security to prevent outbursts. It always had people dressed like a wedding or a funeral, each side either for the victim or the perpetrator.

Not tonight. Instead, it looked like a party box at a Super Bowl game. Somebody had set up a keg of beer. There was a snack table. A dozen or so people milled about in street clothes. When the curtains opened, cheers went up in the audience.

"Is this even possible?" He wasn't certain if she was asking herself or him.

"You really don't think Epstein committed suicide, do you?" He let it go right there. There was no point in torturing the lady. Her end was coming soon enough. This was part of the job he didn't like thinking about, much less talking about.

She grabbed her broach absent-mindedly, still processing the scene in front of her. She looked at the chair, then back to him.

They heard a knock on the glass.

The Governor always looked the same. He looked like a cross between a shoe salesman, an accountant, and a lounge lizard. When he was in his cups, things changed, though. Smithers gathered was most every night. Then he looked worse, like the devil's own version of those things.

He smiled a hello, then tapped at his breast pocket, indicating Smithers' next task.

As the Governor went around to the side door, Smithers withdrew a folded paper.

"I have here a commutation of your execution. You'll still serve life, but next week just before your Execution Day the Governor will announce that now is a time for healing. You can live."

The Governor entered the room. Smithers finished, "It's the best deal you're ever going to get."

She ignored him and instead stared down the Governor. "What do you want, George? Another child to rape? Maybe some more disabled kids ramped up on crank and PCP fighting to the death so you and your cronies can bet on them?"

Now it was the Governor's turn to step back, but Smithers noticed that he recovered as quickly as she did.

Smithers wondered if he had the right person in custody.

"We need to know where the rest of the tapes are, Bev," he said, "You give us the tapes; this all goes away."

"You're going to put this in writing?"

"Right here," he took the paper, "You tell me, I'll sign it. Smithers can witness. It'll be on the Attorney General's desk come first light."

She sat, she actually sat down in the electric chair.

"I have your word."

The Governor nodded somberly, or at least as somberly as he could given the circumstances, "There's nothing in this for me or you if the tapes go away. Even if you come out and try to blackmail me, nobody will believe you. Or hear you for that matter. You have my word."

She considered, toying with something in her pocket.

"Let me see the paper."

The Governor put it on a clipboard, started handing it to her, then stopped.

"The tapes?"

"Sign it first, asshole."

The Governor signed, gave it to Smithers who witnessed it. Now the Governor held it from her again.

"Your turn. Sign it and it all goes away. Where are they?"

"My lawyer's office," she took the clipboard, "in his safe. Like that'll do you any good anyway. You didn't say I had to deliver them, only tell you where they were."

She began signing, humming a happy tune.

"Great," the Governor said. The two men began strapping her in. She had no time to protest. "Let's get this over so we can hit some clubs."

The Governor held her shoulder as if saying goodbye to an old friend.

"But you said."

"Politicians say a lot of things, sweet." The Governor obviously was trying to impersonate Castler. "Your little mind doesn't believe everything it sees now, does it? Poor dear."

"But I'm not prepped. My head should be shaven. I should have had a last meal."

"That'll just make it more entertaining," the Governor said, taking the clipboard back.

He took the commutation letter off and slowly ripped it into pieces, obviously savoring every moment. He dropped it on the floor. Somebody else could clean it up. Such things were beneath him.

"I really wish I could take a picture of this." He said, then smiled again. "Keep it in my special album. But tut-tut," he wagged his finger. "Taking videos and pictures of bad things is a naughty thing to do. I think you know that now, or you will in a minute or two."

"You don't think I have more papers?" She asked, "You think that was all?"

The Governor got out the cap, started to blow the dust off of it, then changed his mind. The dust would be better.

She continued.

"You don't think I mailed myself videos, audio? Put things, things you don't want to come out, in a safe deposit box only I know where?"

Smithers helped the Governor get the ankle contacts wet. They started attaching them to her ankles.

The Governor stood.

"We only have eighteen people here, the witnesses for the execution," He said, "Oh, I could have easily brought in a hundred. What was your final death toll – at least the ones we know about? Eighty-four, wasn't it? Yes, yes, I could have filled the room up several times over."

"George, I'm giving you this last chance. Don't do the wrong thing." She said.

They began applying the cap.

"Sadly, though, I had to limit it to those I could trust with absolute secrecy." He said. "See that lady there?"

He pointed to a frail lady in the gallery. She didn't have a plate or a cup. Instead, she stared into the execution chamber as if looking into hell itself.

"That's my sister." The Governor said, "You don't know. You wouldn't know. Adopted. She's had a hard time with drugs. That's how she lost her two kids."

"It could ruin your career," she added.

"And that's how you ended up with them, at your home, under your care, in your program. I believe they were numbers thirty-nine and forty, at least by our count."

"George."

If he heard her he didn't indicate it. Instead, he went over to the switch.

"They were two that you burned alive in the incinerator. Any last words?"

Smithers could see Bev's body tense. She looked around the room, then out into the audience. As she observed them observing her, her body relaxed. Her smile returned. She was the lady in charge.

"Of course," she said, as if she were giving a prepared speech for the local Rotary Club. "This all reminds me of a little girl I was counseling once. She had a lot of difficulties adjusting and was dealing with PTSD from an absolutely horrible upbringing."

She looked off as if remembering the moment. She nodded to herself, at least as much as she could.

"I always tried to counsel them, you know." She smiled wistfully. "Every so often one would take to it, make good, end up with a scholarship or become a doctor or whatnot. These are our victories. I cherish those. They are so precious."

She turned to look at them.

"But she did not. So I took to more aggressive therapy using the cattle prod and slow acid burns. Eventually skin flaying. I kept hoping beyond hope that it would take. Poor thing. I do love the little ones," she nodded, "and then, sadly, one day it looked as if it wasn't going to work out. I remember quite clearly her telling me that God loves me and no matter what I did, there was always a chance for Heaven for all of us."

"Castler," Smithers hated interrupting, but she had to be reminded that this couldn't go on forever.

"You know what I told her?" Now Beverly became fully happy, "I told her to go fuck herself, that's what. Then I threw her in the wood chipper. She made the nicest sounds."

She looked at the Governor and Smithers, her smile still there.

"You can all go fuck yourselves, and I'll see you in hell."

Electrocution was not painful. Beverly remembered reading that somewhere. It was true.

Of course, to those in attendance, her eyes popped from her skull, her head caught fire, she thrashed around. Her body tightened into a rock each time the switch was thrown. From the outside, she made quite the sight, thrashing in pain. But from the inside, nothing. The audience was allowed in, each one taking a turn at the switch. She voided her bowels, her bladder. She began to smoke, a hotdog left on the griddle too long.

To Beverly Castler, there was a click, a bright light, and all was gone.

She had been turned off.

Silence.

Her eyes opened. There was no choir or heavenly singers, not that she expected one. No devil waited with a pitchfork. No flames. No clouds.

Instead it was Fleetwood Mac.

A bright placard sat on a table announcing "$20 Margarita Mondays!" and several other mixed drinks, all fruity with bright colors. There was music, people talking all around her.

The table was small, square, made of fake wood. She sat in one chair. Two others were empty. As she looked around, she saw a bar. On one side of the bar was a large glass window. Beyond the glass she could see large commercial airplanes pulling in and out of the gates.

People were crowding in, milling about, and crowding out. Almost all had roller luggage. In the background some pop singer of a hundred years ago sang about pain and loss. There was somebody making a gate announcement. A large paper banner hung over the bar. It read, "WINKIES NEWARK, THE BEST LITTLE BAR IN JERSEY!!!!" Underneath, another sign said, "TRIVIA NIGHT!"

"Who you got to screw around here to get service?" She heard from beside her, off to the back.

Glancing back, there were a couple of middle-aged women. They glared back at her.

Excuse me, she wanted to say, I just got executed. Very sorry to bother you. Assholes.

She turned around to the bar again.

Beverly Castler didn't go to heaven. Beverly Castler died. She didn't go to hell. She was not reincarnated. Instead, she ended up in an airport bar in fucking Newark, New Jersey.

The day had really driven off a cliff.

02

The Ride

FOR LEM, HIS DAY ENDED IN BEING ABDUCTED BY DRUG RUNNERS in a magic truck full of corncobs and cocaine. It didn't seem right to Lemuel Rickenbacker that it started with desperately wanting to boil the children in hot oil, but it did. Perhaps that was the punishment. There was also the matter of why anyone would want 24,000 pounds of chicken beaks and an assortment of items including a pile of rusty tricycles and three pairs of brand-new Canadian Sauna Pants.

For Lem, his day ended in being abducted by drug runners in a magic truck full of corncobs and cocaine. It didn't seem right to Lemuel Rickenbacker that it started with desperately wanting to boil the children in hot oil, but it did. Perhaps that was the punishment. There was also the matter of why anyone would want 24,000 pounds of chicken beaks and an assortment of items, including a pile of rusty tricycles and three pairs of brand-new Canadian Sauna Pants.

Since getting off the city bus late that morning, two thoughts fought for dominance in Lem's brain. He found the fight pleasantly distracting. They were, "Now they're going to get it. I'll boil them in oil" and "Remember that it's the pain that purifies." From time to time, as the ideas battled, he interjected into the fight prayers of thankfulness and contrition to the Lord.

Of course, anybody who knew Lem knew that he wasn't going to boil anyone. He'd be lucky to make it from the bus stop to the front door of the home without stopping several times to rest and hope the pain would go away. But he learned a long time ago. When bad thoughts came, he'd take them inside, exaggerate them, then pray the bad feelings away until they didn't concern him anymore. He thought of it as inoculating himself from evil.

He wasn't much to look at, that was true. He wouldn't be getting any dates. He had just turned twenty-four. His skin was patchy black. He was underfed to the point of looking like a concentration camp victim. His wiry, thin hair did not begin to cover the big surgical scar across his scalp, he shook at odd times, and his face was pocked with acne scars.

But that wasn't the worst of it. The worst of it was that he required crutches and braces, his lifelong friends, to get around at all. Even then, movement was difficult. At age three, an accident had given Lem an Acquired Brain Injury that left him with Lower Body Spasticity. That was a fancy way to say, "Use the crutches if you want to move at all. Even then, the more you move, the more unbearable the pain will be for the rest of your life. Would you like some pain pills?"

Lem found that he did. He found that he liked them. The accident that left him crippled as a child and in the foster care system also led him to get hooked on hard drugs by age twelve. They threatened him with institutionalization at age fourteen, a call that was probably a good one on their part. By his mid-teenage years, he'd finally accepted that it was either die or suffer, and he preferred suffering. He slowly made it out of active addiction. He got into a program. When Lem finally graduated high school at nineteen, he'd already begun his lifelong mission. He was going to help as many other troubled kids as he could.

If he could only make it to the house. Boil in oil. Embrace and accept the pain. Thank you God for being with me. Thankfulness. Grateful. Pain. Oil. He could do this. Repeat the mantra. Inoculate.

He got there. He got the door open. Leaning and almost falling inside, he yelled, "Sophie! Sophia Blackwell! Get your lazy behind out here!"

He hated using such language, but the kids were fighting last night, and the group session went terribly. He'd even used the word "damn" once, and he almost never did that. They needed to have a talk, right now, fix whatever was going wrong. His morning trip to the juvenile detention center was eye-opening. Something needed changing, that much was obvious. She was his partner. It was up to them to fix it.

"Sophie!" He heard nothing. He shook his head. "Sophia Blackwell!" Please Lord, not now. Stabbing pain shot along the outside of his right leg. "Sophie?"

He almost fully collapsed on the floor, instead leaning desperately against the doorframe. He tried to recenter.

She did this. He loved Sophie, but she did this. It was always the right thing, and he always hated it when she did.

Sophie was his work partner, the other live-in aide, just friends, at least for now, helping these kids, and she did this.

He knew. She was on one of her walkabouts.

Every so often Lem would get home and Sophie would be gone. Never when the kids were there, heavens no. She was responsible. It was usually in the mornings, and it was once or twice a month.

When it first happened, he didn't know what to do. Did she run away? Should he wait? Should he call? Should he notify the authorities? So he did nothing. Eventually she came home. By the third or fourth time she did it, he began seeking her out. Soon, he learned how to find her. She left. He went to her. That was the way it was done. It became a thing for them.

He never knew if he was supposed to go after her or not, if she wanted him to. He never knew what he was supposed to do when he found her. Usually they would walk a bit. Sometimes they'd just sit by the river. He would try saying things. He would ask questions. She didn't ignore him – she was much too kind for that – but it never seemed like he was doing much, helping much. They'd just sit, maybe chat idly, maybe not, and eventually head back to the home.

It hurt. All of that walking about hurt. Yes, it was a selfish thought, but he had to own it if he ever wanted to be inoculated. It hurt. It hurt to find her. It hurt to walk with her. His joints and legs ached. He had to stop, rest, and go on again. It was sometimes a half hour or an hour until he found her.

It hurt more not to find her.

He never told her about the pain. That would be wrong. She knew anyway. After a few walkabouts and chases, he realized that he felt better afterwards. He began to suspect she did it for him somehow, that the entire pattern was for his benefit.

He looked over his shoulder to the door he was leaning on. There was no point delaying. It was either stop this pattern of self-pity or leave now.

He managed to turn around and head out back the way he came.

It took a half hour of grimacing, struggling, suffering, and occasional embarrassed moaning. He'd made it across the yard, across the busy highway, and into the abandoned lot beyond. From there, there were really only three destinations: the river, the park, or the bridge. A time for choosing.

The old tractor-trailer was parked dead center of the undeveloped lot.

It lingered half-way to all three destinations. He forced himself to make it there. It would be home base. No groaning or yelling, he thought. The more he vocalized the pain the more it controlled him. He would never let that happen again. Remember, it's the pain that purifies, he thought again. Too little pain led to rot. Life was suffering, and that was fine.

Oil.

He felt calmer. He reached the back of the trailer and leaned against it. Time to take stock. Which destination? Could he make it to any of the three?

Then he heard the shuffling, the quiet clanging from inside the tractor.

She's in the cab, he thought, he knew; although he didn't know why. Sophie had broken into somebody's property. This was a first. Should he break in also? Should he just call out? What now, brown cow? Lem started off one way, then another, then back to his first choice,. He moved along as best he could, clanking and rattling like a broken-down ghost looking for a house to haunt.

He made his way around the side to the front. He heard movement in there again. Could be somebody else. Why was it her? Why did it have to be her?

But he knew. He knew the way she moved, the way she fidgeted when bored. He could smell her perfume, for goodness sakes.

Entering the truck would be breaking the law. How could Lem ever counsel these kids and help them find their way if he was out breaking into trucks? And why was she in there, anyway? That's not like her. She set a much better example than he ever did. Sophie was his hero.

There were hard rules in life, and Lemuel Rickenbacker was not the type to break in or steal from people. Not anymore. Never again. Yet his coworker and friend was in there. He was out here. If he called, would she even respond? Perhaps he should just stay here, hovering about, wobbling, until she came out? Lemuel Rickenbacker, truck scarecrow.

He leaned up against the tractor, whether that was the plan or not, simply because he couldn't continue standing. He felt the tremors. He'd pushed far too hard today. Things were going to get very bad. He might not be able to walk tomorrow, but he had to. They needed him. The kids.

Enough with the selfishness. Tomorrow would come when tomorrow was good and ready. He tested the door latch.

Unlocked.

If it was unlocked, he wasn't breaking and entering, and he wasn't about to steal anything. If his friend was there, he was going after her, and that was that. That had to be okay.

He opened the door and began the long process of getting inside.

The interior was clean and shiny. It smelled like leather and chrome polish. He almost fell out trying to get in. It was slippery, sparkly, pristine, pretty, complex, masterful. Rich. Once in and the door shut, he thought again how amazing it was that people could drive, that these trucks had so many controls and could haul things so far. It was an amazing time to be alive. Stay thankful, Lem.

Shutting the door behind him made it darker, foreboding.

Sophie sat between the two seats, her chin in her hands, staring out across the lot towards the river. She looked at if she were doing some math problem or there was some chess move she was planning but not sure of.

If she saw him, she didn't show it.

He looked left and right out of the cab. As usual with her, there was nothing to be seen, no complexities of chess to be considered, only whatever was inside her, puzzle unsolved.

"So this is new," he finally said, "getting into a truck."

"Why did you come find me, Lem?" She turned to him and his blood ran cold. "Why did you come find me here, in the truck? I thought you were still in town."

"JD let out early," he said. "Sophie, somebody owns this truck. You can't be here. We could get in trouble."

She went back to studying the empty lot. She gripped the spiral notebook she always carried that held her art. He waited. She finally turned again.

"I don't want you. Here. Now. I don't want you here at all. You don't know what you're doing."

"Maliki is going to spend some time in prison; that's something I know." He thought distracting her might help. "This was his third felony, and he regularly skips sessions and school. I think we might lose him. The house was a mess this morning. Susan's pregnant. Again. I found pot. Again."

All this, he knew, would bother her. It bothered him a great deal. This was their work and they loved it. It was hard, awful.

She didn't take it up. Instead she said, "Lem, I'm running away. That's why I'm here. It's time for me to move on."

"But...what?" he heard her, but he couldn't understand. "You're here, in this truck? You know these people? What about the home? What about helping out kids? Our job? What about…."

"I believe in what we're doing, Lemuel," she held his hand. "Really, I do. I want to continue. But I'm in a rut. It's my fault we're having all of these problems. The only way out is to leave, head out, take a chance, roll the dice. I've done all that I can. I want to grow. I've become a rerun. I think I'm becoming part of the problem. I'll never do that."

"But…" Surely he could say something. Some words would come forth. He began rocking back and forth, looking around, a caged animal. Come forth, words!

"The truck." was all he got out.

"No, I don't know these people," she said. "My plan was to introduce myself, hitch a ride somewhere, anywhere. So far, the plan's not working out very well."

She looked at him, a disappointment.

She let go and went back to staring.

"I also saw the doctor." He had no idea why he was confessing to her but he knew that he had to tell her if she were truly leaving. "They say I'm stuck with these," he shook a brace to indicate his point, "I'm not progressing any more. They offered more pills. Of course I said no. They say I might actually get a bit worse."

They'd used the word "bedridden", but he wasn't about to say that. He was explaining, not seeking pity.

"My goodness, Lem!" She held his face. "Why didn't you say so? I'm so sorry."

"I didn't mean to say it that way, exactly," the words were still fumbling around in his brain. "Didn't know if I'd tell you at all, really. Probably should have kept it to myself."

She let go of his face and went back to the stare, but this time she didn't mean it. She looked like she was beginning to say goodbye to the parking lot instead of meditating on it.

Still staring, she said, "Tell me what I can do to help. Let me help you."

He thought. He struggled. Was it self-centered to just blurt out what he wanted? Was he manipulating her with his confession? Lord, I don't know what I'm doing, he prayed. Please help me.

His words came out again.

"We'll go back, me and you, make it back home. We still have a couple of hours before the gang arrives. We can talk through it. Please, Sophie, come with me."

She nodded. She gave a very small smile. She looked down and shrugged. Her smile got bigger and she gave up the parking lot.

"Okay Lem. I'll come with you. We can work it out," she said, "but we're not making it very far, I'm afraid."

"Why not?"

She handed him a clipboard. It was the manifest. He remembered that trucks had to have lists of things they were hauling.

He glanced down through it. Chicken beaks, twelve tons. Used tricycles, quantity 18. Three pairs of Canadian Sauna Pants. Four sacks of…

"What a strange shipment."

"Keep reading."

Half-dozen swing sets. Eighty-three air fryers. Forty-six pounds of goat fur. There it was: two hundred kilos of cocaine.

"Oh," he was defeated.

"Yeah, oh," she repeated, "with that much coke, somebody's sure to know we're inside here. This truck might be watched constantly."

"But why would anybody in their right mind list contraband on a manifest?"

"Yeah, Lem. That's what bothers me even more. Why would they?"

"You know, come to think of it, it was always weird seeing this truck. Sometimes it was here, sometimes not. I never saw a driver. I never saw it coming or going, and why would you park a truck, especially with this cargo, out in the open? Even if it were watched? Was it unlocked? Unlocked?"

She nodded.

"I saw the driver," she said, "a couple of times. And the truck leaves every week exactly at this time."

"Which," he said, finally putting it all together, "is why you're here."

They heard yelling in the distance. Talking.

"I think that's him," he said. "We should leave before he gets here. Maybe it's somebody else. I don't know."

She said nothing. He took that as a no.

He had no argument. He might be able to make it out, but he needed to start like right now.

"Sophie, we need to go. Sophie."

Nothing.

"Sophie?"

"There are some things that you don't know, Lem. Some things I need to tell you."

"You want to do our chat, our thing, right now? Ok, then, let's do it right now," he said. They would die, but they would chat. Made as much sense to Lem as anything else.

Maybe the only way out was going inside more.

"Get back here," he body-shoved them both into the sleeper portion of the cab. At least that way they would be out of sight. "This is very bad. Shhh!"

They were both mostly lying down, him in front, her behind. Still, she peered around him and out of a crack in the privacy partition between the sleeper portion of the truck and the cabin.

"It is. There are two of them, Lem," she said. "They both look armed."

"Out of ideas, Sophie."

She considered.

"He's not here yet." She placed her hand on his shoulder. "How about I'll run off, out the passenger side? They'll chase me and you can go the other way. You can do this."

Lem was not a violent man, but he really wanted to hit her, maybe poke her with his finger, give her a good Indian Burn. Pinch her. What was wrong with Sophia Blackwell that she had to drag him into these things? Just last week it was a surprise spring cleaning.

He pulled his braces and crutches the rest of the way in, out of sight. He tried to make himself small.

"No, I am NOT." If he were standing or could stamp his feet he would have done so. "That is not going to happen. That is never going to happen, Sophie. It's just me and you, and we live or die together. I won't hear otherwise. I'm not leaving you."

She cleared her throat and he was suddenly very afraid of what she would say next.

But she said nothing. Instead she let out a long breath in a huge sigh, a gust of regret.

Now he'd done it. He'd laid the law down with her and he'd never done that before. There were to be repercussions. The fear came back. The thoughts started fighting inside him again.

He could feel her looking at him in the inside gloom. The door opened.

He could feel a light breeze. Noon was turning out to be pleasant. He could smell flowers.

She jerked. Please God don't yell or struggle, he thought with horror. He was between her and the cabin, but all she really needed to do was yell. Game over. She could probably come up with some kind of trade where they'd sell her into slavery and he could go free. She was like that. She might try. He didn't think it would work. Not with all of that in the trailer.

She didn't. She jerked, pushed forward on him a bit, gave up, jerked and pushed a bit again, but he could sense her struggle inside, her lack of faith. She didn't know. She couldn't decide. She gave up.

Only one man got in, the driver. It was good. Perhaps?

He began shivering beside Sophie, his muscles protesting and threatening mutiny. Please don't seize, Lemuel, he thought. He said a quick prayer and calmed himself. It seemed to work. The tractor trailer started up. He managed to lean forward to peer through the door into the driver's cabin without banging his head or seizing.

He supposed they would both end up in Mexico, in the desert, shot through the head and left in a shallow grave. He saw that on TV once. Or maybe Sophie could be sold into slavery and they would stick him in an old refrigerator and dump him at sea. He also saw that once. The refrigerator didn't stay down. They kept shooting it until it did.

Lem watched too much TV. To distract himself, he tried to pay close attention to the driver. Maybe there was some clue to how to get out of this. Maybe the man did too many drugs, or drank too much coffee and had to stop to go to the restroom. His mind ran round and round, chasing its own tail in a whirlwind. They could make a run for it, or a hobble for it. Get out somewhere in public, somewhere with a crowd. Whatever. But he wouldn't hurt the man.

As he studied the driver, something even stranger happened.

The truck pulled out of the old lot onto the road in front of the house. Waiting at the stoplight, the man began whistling. Claire De Lune, Lem thought. They started going through the oceanside tunnel.

The driver pulled *back* on the steering wheel, not left or right, but *back*.

It wasn't supposed to work that way. Steering wheel? Pulling back is what you did in airplanes, not trucks. It shouldn't do that.

And then, slowly but surely, the nose of the truck began bouncing off the payment. The truck was riding on the bumpiest road ever. The driver was pulling the truck off the pavement.

These words did not work together.

Lem swallowed hard, looking around the cabin from his hidey-hole. Everything else looked like a truck, or what Lem saw in movies as a truck. It certainly wasn't a plane. As he looked around, the truck left the pavement.

Left the pavement. Completely. A truck. The words were still not working. Round and round we go. Hang on, Lem!

The nose just came up, like the ugliest ginormous airplane ever, heading directly for the roof of the tunnel.

And then they were through it. The truck took off and flew directly through the rock, the water, then completely breaking free of everything.

The sky. Lem saw the sky.

There was just sky in the windshield, puffy clouds, the sun. A bird flew by. They were pointed straight up. They were flying out into outer space. In a truck.

Lem was in a spaceship, or maybe it was a spacetruck, he thought. Do they have spacetrucks? Or were they all ships?

Round and round.

Lem saw the driver grip both hands on the steering wheel hard as the sky darkened. He slowly lost his battle with his muscles. He rolled back to collapse on Sophie. She was viciously shaking him, trying to be quiet yet needing to know what was going on.

That was a good question, he thought. What was going on?

The sky turned black.

03

A Bad Day

THEY WEREN'T IN OUTER SPACE. Lem found that very important. Perhaps they never were.

He was suffering delusions. Had to be.

There was a thump. They hid in the darkness of the sleeping area, in a few minutes another thump, and then they were lying flat again. It felt to Lem like they'd been driving up the steepest hill possible and, once topping it, dropped back to the flat road ahead.

Lem prayed. Please don't let this be some new symptom. He would accept it if it were. It would make helping the kids tougher. He could accept visions and hallucinations. If that's what he needed, he wouldn't be so selfish.

Where were they? Carefully he went back to peeking through the gap between the sleeping partition and the cab. After shaking him several times and getting no response, Sophie had gone silent. She was laying still, perhaps sleeping, perhaps meditating. Plotting.

The driver was wearing a plaid shirt and a ballcap. He didn't appear to be armed but Lem didn't know about such things. Didn't they keep guns in their back pockets or something? On TV the drug people all had machineguns.

The cab looked like he would have guessed. A few snacks. A radio. A GPS. A cellphone on a mount. In the passenger seat there probably was a clipboard, used to be, at least. Sophie took it. Now he was lying on it. Ouch. That would be noticed.

They were on the Jersey Turnpike. Traffic whizzed by, the driver shifting gears and grumbling, trying to keep up. Under the rearview mirror was a little metal science project box, the kind Lem used to see at the electronics store. It had a flip on-off switch and a row of old-fashioned red lights in a row. The lights were off.

Was that a CB? CBs were some kind of radios, though, and Lem had never seen one, so he didn't know. There was nothing to talk into, and the little box was mounted. Perhaps it was some kind of scanner or police radio? He'd read once that drivers had radar scramblers. Maybe that was it.

It was the only thing he saw that he didn't understand. Most everything else made some sort of sense. They certainly weren't in a rocket. He thought about sneaking that clipboard back into the seat before they got caught. As if that would somehow save them.

They pulled into a truck stop. The driver flatulated loudly and began climbing out of the cab, stopping only for a brief second to scratch his butt.

This was their moment. They were at the pumps.

"Where are we?" He felt her head poking around his.

"Truck stop," he whispered. "Not sure if we can get out or not."

"Hmmm," she said nothing, then "What a huge hill."

Without looking back, "Sophia, am I helping you?"

"What do you mean?"

"This thing. The thing we do where you go sit and I come after you. Does that help?"

"Very much, Lemuel. I thought you knew that."

"Very much," he repeated, chewed on it.

"Very much," she gave him a peck on the cheek. "Very much." A third time, "But you know, I can't tell you why. I don't know. Can you believe that?"

"I can. Same."

"Take a rest," she patted him again. "You've been over-exerting."

"Me? I'm okay. Just a bit tired." Should they make a break for it?

"I know better," she nudged him again. "Let's stay. He won't be inside long."

He cleared his throat, shifted a bit uncomfortably, "I'm never truly ok. You know that, more than anybody, I think."

"I do," she took a second. "None of us are. You know that."

As foretold, they promptly heard the driver returning. They moved further into the darkness, listening to the man clamoring up.

They pulled out and the road began to get monotonous again – the shifting, the long groaning of the engine. After a while of that, Lem found himself wanting the driver to say or do anything, but the driver looked very intent on his surroundings. The driver had the look of a man who felt that the cars zipping around them may explode at any moment.

Their machine flowed off a ramp and onto a side road. Within minutes they turned off again. The truck began grumbling and snoring its way down a bumpy dilapidated road. Bumpy. Would the driver pull back on the steering wheel again?

Didn't happen.

Round and round.

It never happened. It was important to Lem to remember that.

The driver parked. They all began waiting, although what Sophie and he were waiting for and how long they had was beyond him. He hoped he didn't have to go to the bathroom. And like magic, once he thought that, he had to go to the bathroom.

The parking spot was very small, by a quarry, and more of a grass field than a lot. After a bit, he saw a tall figure approaching through the forest.

It was a priest, in full outfit, as if he'd just left his church nearby and was going for a leisurely stroll. The man began walking towards the truck. The driver smiled and waved. The priest waved back. Old friends.

Then the driver reached up to the mirror and turned on that little box that he'd mounted. The red lights began flashing in sequence from left to right. Pretty boring.

The sun turned off. But Lem was busy thinking that it must be a scanner and wondering what a priest had to do with drug runners and it made no sense that the sun would turn off. He didn't see it, at least at first. Sophia had given up, otherwise he would ask her. He elbowed her.

Things got really weird. It was dark outside, but they weren't really outside, were they, Lem? They were on a large plain of gray sand and black sky. No, not sand, dust, fine dust, like talcum powder. It looked like pictures he'd seen as a kid of the moon. Astronauts bouncing around.

They were on the moon. Had to be. Also Lem had lost his mind. But the delusions kept coming, before Sophie could get beside him, he looked for the priest. Priests don't live on the moon, do they? They didn't have churches there. The moon's far away. Who would come?

But there wasn't a priest. Instead of the priest, there was a giant… insect? A grasshopper wearing a suit of armor? A metal man? Steel bug?

Lem was going to have to see a doctor again. He must have been exposed to some kind of drugs in the truck. His brain injury must be getting awful. Something. He should have paid more attention to the doctors earlier that day. He didn't remember them saying this might happen.

The driver flipped the box off. He felt Sophie at his side.

They were in a grassy spot. It was not the moon. They'd always been, he told himself. There was the quarry, the grass, the forest, just like it always was. There was a priest.

The driver got out again. Thankfully this time without the accompanying sounds and smells. While the priest waited peacefully, Lem heard the back doors open up. He heard some dragging, more complaining, and the doors being slammed shut again.

Dead bodies. The thought came to him and instantly had him mesmerized. If there were dead people back there, and as far as he knew neither one of them had looked in the back, there could be a dozen of them back there, and they wouldn't be on the manifest, would they? But one guy couldn't drag a body around like this. He saw on TV that bodies are too slushy and heavy just to pick them up and carry them. It would be a struggle, even for large man.

But not an insect. Or an angel. Metal bug. Monsters

But it wasn't a body.

The driver appeared holding three boxes. Lem could see that each box was labeled "Canadian Sauna Pants" There was some small lettering that said, "Look and feel Canadian, Instantly!" He thought he saw "magic" but he didn't have time to read the rest.

They seemed like old friends, both smiling, the driver using his free hand to shake. The priest took the boxes, they chatted a bit longer. Laughing, the priest walked off, back the way he came. The driver watched him a bit, waved, then headed back to the cab.

The little box under the rearview mirror remained unlit. They were not on the moon. There were no bodies, no magic. It was all the dull, mundane trappings of life.

Both Lem and Sophie rolled back into quiet solitude as the trip droned on. He'd almost dozed off when they pulled in again.

The driver began getting out, and this time both of them snuck a peek.

Bunch of different vehicles in a lot. Busy. The driver walked towards the door.

"Hamburger Heaven."

It was a restaurant. Lem felt the need to pee almost overwhelm him.

"We know this truck is going back to our home eventually," he told her once the driver was a good ways off. "As long as we can stay hidden we'll end up back home."

He said the words and felt the need to go to the bathroom at the same time. His bladder and his brain were headed in opposite directions. Somebody was going to win.

"Lemuel, I'll talk to you. We'll keep in touch." She spoke quietly, not daring to look at him. "We can even go back to the home and have a good heart-to-heart if you want." She took in a breath. "But I'm not going back. I'm never going back, permanently, at least."

"This is bad," he said, talking about their situation and wishing he were talking about what she just told him, "I want to help, but I don't want to enable you. You shouldn't do this."

Therapy words came out. They were not the right words. Lem had collected many therapy words over the years and always found himself using them when he didn't want to be honest with himself. What was wrong with him? Lately? He'd need to start making a list. There were a lot of things wrong.

Maybe Lem needed his own manifest of problems he was carrying around.

The driver came back. It had only been a minute or two. He couldn't have eaten that fast. He elbowed and manhandled Sophie again. Get back!

The door opened. More whistling. The driver didn't get in all the way. Instead he pulled his wallet out and began rummaging.

"Hi there!"

It was Sophie. She was shouting to the guy. Sophie.

"Why are you doing this?" Lem spoke aloud, in a flat voice. Lem was giving up. He spoke as if they were having the most reasonable conversation ever. Certainly they were not hiding in a truck from who knows whom. Certainly Lem was not getting ready to pee all over himself.

The driver froze immediately, not believing what he'd heard.

So she said it again, "Hi there!" and reaching over him started pulling the partition back.

This time he heard.

"What!" He climbed back in, staring the entire time, slamming the door behind. "Who the hell are you?"

Lemuel stuck his hand out and waved as if saying hi there. "Two. Two of us" He said the words to the ceiling. He didn't want to look at what was coming.

Refrigerators in the ocean. Lem knew.

Keeping them in sight, the driver produced a gun. He did have a gun. Joyous reunion.

Lem and Sophia both struggled with one another, finally reaching a sitting position on the bunk, side-by-side. They were kids on a trip to the zoo. Are we there yet?

He was going to say something, Lem thought desperately. The driver was going to say something awful and they would be tortured to death. They'd end up in that refrigerator, bobbing around, on TV.

Lem tried to smile but he knew he was making an awful face. The only face Lem conjured up was a sideways grin of horrified desperation.

"I'll tell you anything you want to know," he tried to cut the man off before the trouble could begin. "Whatever I can do to help. Whatever we could do. I'll cooperate."

"Hi!" Sophie said it again, bless her, "We're just a couple of kids. I'm Sophia and this is Lemuel. Sorry about the hiding, but we're trying to hitch a ride out of town. Our bad," as if she had a gun pointed at her every day.

"Like I'm going to believe that," the driver snarled at them. "You're Plexis, probably Delta Shard."

Then he looked back to that weird device he had under the mirror and Lem thought the man was arguing with himself. The driver stared them down again.

"Where is the nest pod of the gamma swarm? Are you carrying larvae?"

They both said nothing. Lem wondered if he were very quiet the man would go away.

He did not.

"Klaxon Forty-three?" Lem wondered if these were words, if the guy was actually speaking. "Obfuscated…or destroyed? Think carefully before you speak."

They both stared at each other for a second, each wanting the other to come up with something. Both confused, they turned again to the man.

"And don't lie to me. This is set to kill."

A gun?

A gun would always be set to kill. Lem shook his head. Was Sophie seeing and hearing this? Was Sophie even there?"

"Nexel Five-Bone, Ellipsis. You report to him? He send you?"

This man was going to kill him. This man was crazy, he had a gun, he was selling sauna pants and cocaine, they were at a restaurant, and he was going to kill them. Lem did not have therapy words for this.

Also he had to go pee.

He raised his hand as if he were in elementary school.

"I have to go pee." If they were going to kill them, instead of a cigarette, Lem wanted to pee first. Seemed reasonable enough, as reasonable as anything else lately.

"Hmmm," the man shrugged. As they waited for their death they watched him scratch his chin, deep in thought.

"Don't you believe us?" Sophie asked, "We're just stowaways. From the home. I don't know these questions you're talking about. We don't understand."

He looked again at the box, then back to them.

He grunted.

"I do believe you, that's the problem."

Jerking back and thrashing around, Lem began seizing. What timing. The lights went off. The lights came back on. Repeat. Reality flickered as he fought to come back, to stay back.

It was only a few seconds, he thought, but he never really knew. Could have been an hour. Maybe it was only a second. Nexel Five Bone.

What a really inconvenient place to do that, he thought. He awoke, slowly opening his eyes. Fighting himself, he was scared by the face of the driver just inches away.

"Is he okay?" the driver asked.

"He does that," he heard Sophia answer. He couldn't get the words working again, although he fought to make the jaws work.

He moved his mouth up and down as they watched, but nothing came out.

He grabbed them. "How about if I go," he finally said, "I should call a doctor, maybe get some help or rest. I don't want to be a burden. I need help."

If we can split up, he thought, I can call the police. Whatever we do, split up, contact authorities; somebody had to. The driver was concerned; play off of that. It was their only hope.

The driver said something very strange, not to Lemuel but to Sophia.

"Who's going to take care of him?"

"I. Am. Okay." Lemuel was going to get really angry. This was enough. Just shoot me already. "Don't need help. Thank you, but no thank you."

Sophie considered this. "I will," she said before Lem could assemble more words. He was sleepy. He was always sleepy afterwards.

He started dozing off. He pinched himself. He hit himself on the legs, making them hurt even more.

Still keeping eyes open. Still having to pee.

"Does he need anything? Medicine?" The driver asked.

She gently shook him, the way you might peacefully wake a loved one. She was concerned.

"No, he's fine." She said. "That was just a little one. He pushes too hard sometimes, that's all."

He did not want this. Lem did not want this at all.

A loud honk, they all looked. Another tractor-trailer pulling in. Already 20 or 30 vehicles were in the lot.

"I want to go home." There was nobody to say it to, but he said it anyway, "We want to go home."

"Please don't kill us," she immediately added.

"Hmmm…" The scratching again, then, "interesting. You know what? I'm not going to kill you. Why don't you kids run along? Beat it. We'll call it even."

He put the gun away.

"Why not just stay here, Lem?" she asked. "If he'll have us, why not just continue our trip? Could we stay?"

Because he might be lying, Lem thought but didn't say.

"Not opposed to it," the driver answered before he could. "Honestly, it'd be good to have some company. Might learn a thing or two about truck-driving, see the countryside. Driving's a great career. You should consider it."

"But," Lem said. "But we." Finally, "I need to go to the bathroom. We should leave this poor man alone. We've surprised him enough, Sophie. We're being very rude."

"Maybe," she nudged him again. "What do you think? We could go with him. That's what I wanted to do all along. How about it, Lem?"

He said it. He had to say it. He didn't want to say it, and there it was.

"But the contra…contraband."

They both looked at him as if he had just made up the word. He knew it was a word. They needed to get this settled, just everybody say it's okay, before anything else. Right now they were in a busy place. Maybe they could scream.

Later, probably not.

"The coke," he said.

"Coca-Cola?"

"Cocaine," he said. Well, there it was, Lem. Sink or swim. You're on the ocean now, bobbing around.

The man began laughing, unable to control his mirth. Lem felt his face turn red.

The driver finally got a hold on himself. "You're not from around here, are you?"

More laughter.

"No," he didn't know what was so funny.

"It's not a problem at all." The driver calmed down. He tried to look serious. "Cocaine? Funny. Don't worry a minute about it. You have my word."

He began smiling again but did not laugh. He put his hand to his heart.

Lem didn't know if he liked this guy or hated him. Hate was bad, so he decided to like him.

Liking the man was going to be difficult.

He certainly wasn't going to bring up the moon to either one of them.

"But I can't take you both," the driver said, "there'd be no place to sleep, right? And who's going to take care of him?"

He knew what the man meant, he meant Lemuel. Lem gritted his teeth. "You've got it wrong. I'm here for her. I'm helping her."

"That's right," she said, and relief flooded over him. "We've only been gone a few hours. How about just giving us a ride back home? We'll be quiet the entire way. We can pay you."

"I really don't need caring for." Nobody was listening to him.

"'Fraid I'm not going back, not for a good while," the driver just ignored him.

Could he trust this man?

"What are our chances?" Sophia asked, "you care about our safety, right? You want to be nice, right? This looks like a tough place. Could we make it back home, hang out here for a while? What would you do?"

The driver shuffled. He'd been found out.

"Frankly, young lady, odds are something bad is going to happen to you both, even if you come with me. This isn't the nicest place. Can't lie about that. Me, I'm just a working stiff. But your choices don't look so good, sorry to say."

"Out we go." Lem was done talking to this man and fought with his crutches and braces.

As he opened the passenger door, the driver continued.

"If it helps any, try not to talk to anybody," he looked at the clipboard with the manifest, "and be sure not to mention anything in the back, none of it. Keep your mouth shut, call the cops, call him an ambulance. It'll be alright."

Lem didn't believe him for a second. He didn't think Sophie did either.

The door fully opened and Lem swung out on it like it was a horizontal seesaw. Wheeee.

"Maybe," the driver finished, just as Lem's muscles gave up and he fell face down into the lot, his head hitting the pavement and his crutches all around.

"I'll get him," he heard Sophia say, and as fast as he could, he began gathering himself together. He felt a knot on his forehead. There was no blood, so that was good.

"Got it," he pulled himself to standing as she exited. "Just a little tumble."

"Sure you're okay? Sure I can't call somebody for you?" The driver peered across the seat and the open passenger door.

"Don't worry about it, we're fine. Typical day for us," Sophie waved at the man. He eventually smiled back, shut the door, and started the truck back up.

But he didn't leave.

"What a guy, didn't think he would be so nice," Lem said. He wasn't lying, but he wasn't comfortable saying it, either, "Let's get to the road, hitch a ride. He said it wasn't good here."

"I can see you swaying."

"Just kinda relaxing," he tried to sway even more, on purpose, ridiculously so, as if he had invented the exercise and was running seminars to help other ABI patients with Lower-Body Spasticity by swinging around on their crutches. Follow me for more tips.

"They have seats inside, food, a bathroom," she decided not to continue, instead walking ahead of him, into the restaurant. She walked very slowly, allowing him to keep up, but she refused to engage more.

If she went, he would go. Maybe Sophie knew that. Maybe she always knew that.

Lemuel Rickenbacker was defeated. Yet again Sophie needed help and yet again he was going to be there for her.

Dead Reckoning

THE DEAD AREN'T GONE. The dead aren't forgotten. The dead aren't even dead.

"Welcome to the first day of the rest of your life!"

Beverly looked up. The man was tall, thin, maybe six feet six. He had dark, wavy hair. Green eyes. He looked about thirty. He held himself with military posture. He was some kind of cop. Had to be. He had the biggest smile she'd seen. She briefly thought he was going to sell her a condo.

He did a perfect dubstep. He stuck his right elbow towards her face and waggled it. Sitting down across from her. He continued to smile and without missing a beat, said, "You're Beverly Castler. Howdy, I'm Mack Azure. We're going to be working together. You're going to have more fun than you ever thought possible."

If he'd been reading from a card, it would have been just as persuasive.

Then he wrinkled his nose and sniffed. "As I understand it, we do not exchange bodily fluids, at least not yet, and simply name ourselves. I am to present myself as a resource. Let me assure you," he points at her with three fingers. "You will enjoy this."

Now he seemed really serious.

He rubbed his hands together. His mood instantly went from ludicrously happy to serious to no expression at all.

She thought she must be confused.

"Happy? You're happy? Who are you? Where am I?"

"Winkies, of course. Congratulations for moving out of the DIM levels! Took me four thousand cycles. Slow learner, what are you going to do? My burden, I'm afraid. You're ahead of the game. The right people have taken notice."

He tapped his temple to emphasize the point. She had done something right.

"People? Is this heaven? Hell? Is this punishment?"

"Heav….Fearfully no. Ha!" He was happy again as he pulled on his nose. "You are joking. We don't do the judgmental stuff here. We found that there was far too much arguing involved. Immanuel Kant, oh dear. What a pain that man was. They're still talking about him. Instead, in whatever life you've just had, you're already judged by the people you interact with, right? So we use that. It's DIM. D-I-M. Death, Impact, and Meaning. That's your three categories. How people view those three things determines where you're headed next. Very simple. Max out any of them, plus-or-minus, end up here at Winkies. Max out all three at once? Management. But now you're at Winkies, so we've got a lot of work to do."

"Death, Impact, Meaning," she said, "DIM. I was a DIM level. I was DIM. A job. This is a job? So if I had a really awful death, or a terrific impact on others, or held a really meaningful life, I come here?"

"As judged by others? That's right! But you have to be really outstanding, though. You have to be one-in-a-million in the category or beyond, good or bad, then you come here. 'Extremes make the means,' they say. 'Four to the tenth means you're spent.' You'll learn. You get to see me. Or at least somebody like me. Did you expect somebody in a boat? Spirit animal? Sorry. It's been a while. I'm a bit rusty. I can do voices if you like."

"So I had a horrible death, and now I'm here because it was so terrible? I'm slave labor?"

"No, your death was quite boring, actually. Sorry to say that. Thems the breaks. You had a tremendously horrible impact on others, though, that's why you're here. Congratulations! Of course, if you had a tremendously good impact on others, you'd be here too, but you'd probably have a different partner. One way or the other, we don't care. Say, do you paint? Compose music? I've dabbled in poetry. Always wanted to learn calligraphy."

She shook her head no.

"A tragedy," he continued, "but we'll see what we can do. You're the clay we have, not the sonnet one might like. It's all good."

"You're serious about this? You're honest? This isn't just more games from the Governor?"

"Serious? Yes, but honest? Very rarely! In fact, most of the time I'm lying. But that's for me to know and you to figure out. Works best that way. Have you ordered yet?"

"You can order?"

"How else would you get service? I'm starving."

He waved over somebody and placed an order for potato skins.

"You DIM levels love your animal flesh, but I figured we could start with roots. Would you like something to drink?"

She held her hand out, not ready to acquiesce, supplicating. as if asking for alms. "So I'm somehow good or bad on this DIM scale and I'm here." She waved it around. "At Winkies. What about all the other dead people?"

"They're all here too, of course," he said, "or someplace else. Just not in Winkies, most likely. I hear the Piña Coladas are incredible. Not yet Happy Hour, though."

He smacked his lips.

She looked up to the TVs overhead and saw a news story. It was the continuation of a story she saw yesterday, before her electrocution.

Before she died.

"So I could just…pick up the phone? Call my friends and have them pick me up? Here I am, Bev, back from the dead?"

"Well you could, of course, and many people try that, don't you know! But it never works."

"I don't understand."

"You see, the more emotionally connected you are to any of these other creatures," he gestured around the airport, "the less your ability to interact with them. So, for instance, the boy who you haven't seen in thirty years would be fine to call, but your…hmmm…Warden, lawyer, or fellow prisoners would not work; never work, in fact, no matter how hard you tried."

"It's just a phone. I don't.….I bet that I'm in one of those NDEs," she said to herself, "Near Death Experiences. I know. I'm having some sort of endorphin overload. Oh dear. You are very strange. I was expecting a light."

"Light? Hmmmm." He scratched his chin. "As I recall, we used to do large campfires. There was a time we were doing strong winds and thunderstorms. You are worrying far too much, Bev. Can I call you Bev? Good. Really, what does it matter? I'm here. You're here. Watch."

Mack stood up from the table but not all the way. Looking out into the corridor, he waved over an elderly man walking down the concourse.

As the man approached, Mack sat back down. He gestured to Bev as if he were giving the old man to her.

"Your name, sir?"

"Frederick," the man said. He stood a little straighter.

"Wait a minute," she almost jumped off the seat herself. "Frederick? Fred Castler? From Des Moines?"

"The one and only!" He'd won a prize.

She stuck her head almost in Mack's face. She pointed over her shoulder with her thumb at the recently arrived man. "Grandpa? That's my grandpa?"

Mack nodded cheerfully. "Say Fred, do you remember little Beverly?"

"Why sure I do! Little tiny thing. Had this dog named Rex…"

Mack made the hurrying up motion, then patted the man on the arm and sent him off with, "just making a point for my friend here. Very sorry to bother you, sir."

"Young lady," her grandpa said, "I bet you're Beverly, all grown up. We loved you so dearly, your grandma and me. Listen to this man, whatever it is. This has been a fantastic hootenanny. Every day fresh."

He left, patting her on the shoulder and smiling kindly first. Mack looked back at her. She saw the smile again.

"It's been a long time," he said. "He could tell you anything you wanted to know about your young life. That's because neither you nor him are emotionally connected to it anymore. It's allowed."

"But if I picked up the phone to call a current friend…"

"The phone wouldn't work. Or you'd visit their house and instead of a house you'd see an empty lot. The closer you are emotionally to somebody, the less you can know about them. That's one of the reasons they pair you up with folks like me from out of town. I can pretty much know anything about anybody. It's all so tiresome, though. Without social context it becomes so much trivia, random facts. Boring."

"See him?" he pointed to a man in line. "He has a hangnail on his left big toe. Whether that's important or not is beyond my knowledge. It's far, far too tedious to continually correlate. It probably is. He's walking oddly."

"Out of town," she blankly repeated, "You're from out of town. Where you from, Pittsburgh?"

"A bit further than that! Ha! In your time on this ball, haven't you wanted to do something new? Guess what? Today's your day. Lucky you. I'm your new best friend."

"Next you're going to tell me that you're not from Earth."

"Right you are. Top of your class, I bet," he leaned back, continuing to be pleased in their conversation. He wiggled his elbow in her face again.

"Gas giant. Bunch of moons. A good ways off from here, especially for you non-FTL folks. But it was home. Pleasant enough. I had oomphlas."

"So…you're not human?"

"By the Axial Phonons, no! Let's see. I think that to you I would probably look like a cross between what you call an octopus and a hornet. Something flying, stinging, changing colors, having mind control, that kind of thing. Nothing much special. We led a quiet life there, farming mostly."

"I've gone crazy. How could you possibly be sitting here? You're just a person. This is crazy. You're not a squid."

"Oh yes! Forgot about the Universal Sentient Interface! Knew I was forgetting something. USI. We've all got them – at least the creatures in this plane. Never met any that didn't. Sorry about that," he tapped his head. "You just forget about them after a while."

She put her head in her hands. "Couldn't I just have stayed dead?"

"The USI allows sentient creatures to interact. It uses whatever construct works the best for their primitive brains. For you folks? I guess we're at Winkies. It's all quantum nonsense. Looks like a pretty good crowd. I might try the key lime pie. Think it's good?"

"You're going to tell me next I'm in the Matrix, some kind of computer thing, then I'm going to hurt you with my salad fork."

"No, dear Beverly. You are a real person and you are really in Newark. Nothing here is fake or artificial. Here we are. I am also a real creature and I am both here and on my home planet. At least I guess I'm in both places. I also might just be here or somewhere else. There might be many of me. Really don't care much about all those sorts of things. Like I said, you forget about it. Your USI is just there all the time. It just works."

"Sorts of things…" Bev was beginning to feel lost. More lost.

"Location, of course. Once you understand the USI, you understand it really doesn't matter who we are or where we are, even if there are many versions of us. Silly nonsense, that. USI works it all out. We just go about our business, as it were. Locality was always for chumps, don't you think? And don't even get me started about observer-dependent retrocausality. And don't start going on about snails again. We're not getting the escargot. I could go on for hours. In fact, I may have already done so next week. If I do, please remind me."

"I don't know what to think, Mr…"

"Mack! Mack Azure. Call me Mack. Whoa, here come those potato skins! I don't think I can eat all of this. Look at that."

The waiter sat the tray down and Mack slowly began eating, experimenting with the fork.

She shook her head no, but there was nobody she was shaking it to.

She looked at her fork, testing it.

"You're saying somehow it all works out. You're my friend. I shouldn't worry that you're a giant flying octopus and going to eat me."

"Ha ha! You're funny. Why would I eat a coworker?" He waved his fork, "And I'm only about seven of your centimeters across, hardly scary. You're huge. You mentioned something you call 'The Matrix'. You people have those games with the simulations? You have initial computational technology, no? Leisure activities? Where you play-pretend to be other creatures in other, more interesting situations?"

"You mean like The Sims? Or Warcraft? Meta?"

"Exactly," he put his fork down. "Haven't you always wanted to have your Sims interact with your Warcraft people? Well, why the hell not? It's just a matter of programming. And so we are here. It's just more of that. Good! Our drinks are ready."

He thought for a moment, noticing he wasn't getting through.

"Let's see, I believe you can convert units almost painlessly, say from Imperial to Metric, right? I believe you have advanced your translation technology to the point that it's almost invisible. You can convert number systems of completely different societies, correct? You've worked out people can interact simply by talking, no effort required. Same thing. Consciousness is a quantum phenomenon. You see me and I see you. We're here."

A voice came over the intercom.

"For those waiting for the outbound flight to Los Angeles, we regret to inform you that it has been canceled due to maintenance issues. Please stay in the gate area …."

"Oh goodness," he said.

"Oh goodness what?"

"Never mind."

Now it was her turn to lean back, take it all in. She didn't know if she were crazy, dead, crazy and dead, or what, but this was what she had, so this was what she was going to work with.

"Why should I talk to you, Mr. Zack?" she squinted. "As far as I know, you're just some random Joe who came by. Maybe they drugged me and put me here. You're nobody."

"You're not listening, Beverly Castler," he said. "I am Mack. I'm not making any sort of request. I'm telling you. This is the first day of your new job, and I'll be your supervisor. We have work to do. It can be fun… or otherwise. Your choice."

"This DIM shit you keep pushing, let's say that I had the most mundane death ever. My death was not too terrible and not too great. I had a life with zero impact. It didn't mean a lot of good to others nor a lot of bad. I lived completely either without good or bad meaning. I was the ultimate average person. Let's suppose that I was perfectly mid."

"Triple Zero," he said, trying the sour cream and making a face. "Dead Center. Regression to the Mean. They would probably discontinue you. Very bad. That's where most sentient creatures gravitate towards. Civilizations tend to not do much of anything aside from being the most average possible. I imagine that's why it's set up the way it is. The universe must be in balance, so the extremes are rewarded, but all of that's above my pay grade. We all have our small jobs. Now you have yours. Would you like some of the steamed shrimp? What is this 'calamari'?"

She instinctively touched her broach. He took interest.

"Say, is that silver artwork? The design is quite exquisite."

"Seventeenth-Century. I guess you would say that was several hundred revolutions around our local star previously?" She tried to do the translation.

"Beautiful work. Your species has really done a lot with the place since I last visited. Horrible time then. We were lucky to get custom-made pottery. Had to travel for that."

It didn't seem to be a joke. She didn't see cameras. She didn't feel loopy.

"You're going to have to give me a minute, Zack."

"It's Mack. Sure, take your time."

"It's just that everything's changed." She put on the matronly smile, began engaging him as a beloved friend. Working him. She was old and confused. She needed help.

"Has it, really?" he said, "If it helps, it's always been like this. You just didn't know it until now. Would you like to go back? Cycle around again? I can arrange it. I can cycle you. You just can't leave without me. Not yet. But soon. We'll get you there."

"So if I don't listen to you, what are you going to do, zap all my memories or something? Start me off again as a baby? Give me pain?"

She couldn't help thinking of the many children she'd counseled over the years. It was a similar conversation.

"Oh, Bev, we have all sorts of options. Never you mind. Here, take this in."

He reached into his breast pocket and retrieved what looked like a slice of petrified wood.

"It's a slice of the biological computational structure of a species that lives near here, only a few thousand light-years away. They call themselves the…well, it's unpronounceable, sadly. As it turns out, as they gestate and grow, at least the second time, parts of their minds grow organically. Parts they actually remove and deliberately, caerfully shape into beautiful computational crystals. They literally form their thoughts into existence and make them permanent, like a statue."

She held the slice of rock. It had a tremendous amount of intricate detail, she had to admit. In a way it was quite beautiful. She wondered how many other curiosities Mack carried around. She wondered how he got them.

She thought she understood his meaning.

"Is there some sort of test? You're threatening me? If I need to do or perform for you, just tell me what you want. Are you going to make me into a rock? You're a dear, but you are quite…" She looked around the bar; she couldn't be bothered. "Pointless I suppose, even if you are real. A boor."

That was total horse hockey, she knew. It was important to feel things out if they were going to work together, if she was eventually going to master this new system.

Work it, Bev.

"Give me whatever test I have to pass," she said, "right now."

"I can start you on the test, certainly, at least the verbal part," he said, "but if you fail, it's a memory zap and another cycle around. If that's what you want…"

She did, in fact, know nothing. He was correct about that. Mack Azure kept coming up with explanations for things Beverly had no knowledge about. It was important either to get into a rhythm of manipulating him, kindly, having him look out for her, of course, or give it up. Otherwise she'd always be chasing along behind, trying to keep up.

That was never going to happen. She was never going to allow it.

Pity me or destroy me, Mack, she thought, pick one.

"Give it to me," she said. "Let's start."

He crossed his arms in bemused surprise.

"Fine. Your choice. You're now in The Guardians, which I was getting ready to start explaining before you decided to, um, get ahead so quickly. What are the Three Rules of The Guardians?"

Well, she thought, he called her bluff. He wasn't going to coddle her if she acted petulant. Take it in stride. She'd fumbled. She was confused. Grandmas did that.

"I guess that's it for me. You got me. I don't know. Go ahead and get it over with. Do your cycle thing."

She held her arms out, palms up. I'm done.

It was the moment.

He took another drink. He held his glass for a moment, not deciding whether to continue or not, then sat it down.

"Oh my goodness gracious!" He patted his chest as if trying to get something down. He made a snorting sound, pulled on his nose again, "I'd forgotten how much I just love working with primates. The charging, the bluster. The retreat. The sullenness. Bluffing. The grooming each other's egos while gossiping about others. Controlling the flow of ranking information. The posturing to become head of the troupe. Combat. You are all quite precious. I really wish I'd kept more of you as pets. You are inflexible and lack the ability to trust, but we will work with that. We are going to have such fun working together!"

"You're not zapping me?"

Mack almost laughed at her, "Zap you? Cycle? Of course not. I lied. I do that a lot. Already told you that. Helps cut through the social nonsense when necessary. You see, I know you already, Beverly Castler. Not very difficult. You're here. You were taken off-guard. Now you're busy evaluating your circumstances and maneuvering your way to move to the head of the pack. You'll sell me out or kill me if you have a chance, and it'll be in the most pleasant way. Perhaps even clever! I certainly hope you can show me some of the art of the way you do this. I find it endlessly fascinating. Also calligraphy."

"You lied?"

"Of course I lied! Do it all the time. You don't even know where you are, much less what you're doing or what's expected of you. How could you ever pass a test? Now let's get you started on your new job."

He looked at her again. "Unless you want to play more, perhaps you're hungry, or you really want to go back. I'm not a fan of cycling right off the bat. Always seemed a bit slovenly on the part of the trainers to me. It might have taken you a while to get here, but I can accommodate you if you insist."

There was just no controlling this man, creature, whatever it was.

She shook her head no, slowly, watching him.

"Well, that does it then," he said, obviously pleased with her choice, "Let's roll!"

He motioned for a check.

Attention Walmart Shoppers

IF THE AFTERLIFE WAS GOING TO BE SOME KIND OF STUPID, on-the-job training with this ludicrous lunk of lunacy, Beverly was going to have fun.

She had no idea.

"Cop car? We get a cop car?"

Out of the airport they came and into the long-term parking lot they went. Bev had wanted to take the shuttle, of course, but Mack insisted on a long walk, soaking it all in: car exhaust, smelly trash, honking of angry drivers.

He reveled.

"I believe this should give us all the, erm, 'accoutrements' your people would expect," he replied.

They both stood looking at the car, right out of a 1970s TV show. Bev thought it was the most ridiculous thing ever. But hey, when in Rome, right?

"I like it. Do we get badges and guns? Is anybody going to take any of this seriously?"

No, no, and yes. The USI will provide us whatever translation we need, never you mind. I thought this would be the most fun. I have a little pull. But if you like, if it will help, I can get us some authentic period costumes and props. I have several quotations from your cop fiction collection I've cultivated on our walk out. If you don't know any…"

He let the question hang.

"I'm sure I'll be fine. This is great, Mack. This is great, for whatever it is you'll want us doing, I'm sure. It'll be fun. Let's do it."

She tried to imitate the amount of pleasure he was showing. He seemed not to notice her fakery.

"This is indeed fantastic," he rubbed his hands in glee, pointing that she should get in on the passenger side. "I will be your, as they say, senior training partner, I believe. But be assured that I am not ready to retire and do not expect to die violently by the hands of hardened criminals!"

One can only hope, she thought.

He laughed a bit before continuing. "Although you may provide most of the jokes as a comic sidekick as you want. Your discretion, of course. That might be even more pleasant."

"I'll try to keep up," she said, scanning the dashboard, looked normal, looking back to Mack, expecting him to do something. He seemed not to know where he was but enjoying the hell out of it anyway. "What now, Senior Training Partner Mack Azure?"

"Oh, that's me," he looked left and right, still smiling. He smiled like a wolf. "Now we go shopping, of course! Have you done this kind of thing before?"

He started the car and began looking around. Bev was relieved that he had no problems operating a vehicle. Perhaps it was something he put on automatic. She filed that away.

"Shopping? Many times."

"ha HA!" He stopped pulling out. He slapped his leg, "A joke! You are, indeed, the comic sidekick! Maybe you can die a poignant death, saving me as I catch the criminals!"

"Too late, Mack, already died," she studied him as he continued pulling out, then she said, "are you asking if I have done training? Yes, many times. On both sides of the relationship. I was considered quite good, an expert even."

"That is even more fantastic." He did not stop what he was doing but continued to the gate. "Then we shall be, as you say, 'kick-ass'. I will do my best to entertain you as we continue your most serious training."

"We can only hope," she replied, this time aloud, looking out the passenger window. The day was cloudy. Rain might be shaping up.

She was dead.

"You know, Mack, I might be able to teach you a thing or two," she said a few minutes later as they made their way onto the main road. "After all, I live here, or I lived here, very recently. I can help in all sorts of areas you might not expect."

"Amazingly unexpected!" He said, and she was instantly afraid he'd just stop the car in the middle of the highway to continue their conversation.

He did not. Instead he asked. "Do you know much of this 'Bonsai Tree' business? Looks most impressive."

"No."

"How about competitive yodeling? Very folk music."

"No."

"Do you play the, how do they say, the little one, the banjo? Or juggle? Or perhaps perchance river dance!"

"No."

"Any good at tattooing, pyramid building, animal sounds, ritual sacrifice?"

"Not ritual, no. But, I can meow."

"And still no calligraphy."

"No."

He patted her knee. "We have time, young Beverly! Our partnership has just begun! Never you fear!"

They pulled into the Walmart parking lot. She had been expecting something a bit more upscale, but who knew what the hell they were actually looking at.

Parking and getting out, a homeless man approached.

"Wash your windshield, watch your car. Ten bucks," he said. His smile was perfect – not a tooth missing. His hair was just right. Bev thought the man looked like the CEO of a local company. She imagined him sitting that morning in his big chair, losing his job and everything he owned. They gave him bad clothing and a squeegee. They told him to go work the local strip mall parking lot.

Her partner took in none of these inconsistencies. Instead, Mack walked over to the man and looked at him like he was a long-lost friend. He placed his arm outstretched on the upper arm of the man.

"You are very sick. You don't have long to live."

Then Mack dropped his arm and, as if nothing happened, turned and came back.

Watching, Bev saw the man turn to go back the way he came. "I feel awful," he said, shuffling off.

"Come, let us shop!"

They began towards the door.

"You've done training, Bev, so tell me about your toughest training."

She frowned at him, not stopping, glancing back at the homeless guy for a second. Then she picked up the pace and continued mimicking the light attitude.

"Probably when I ran those workshops for Child Protective Workers. I had to be very strict with them. How about you?"

He stopped. Rubbing his chin. They were in the crosswalk, but no cars were waiting. Yet. Standing there.

"Had to be the Bo'dinqul'inniukuk." He looked at her and nodded, as if she already knew.

She nodded towards the door and they continued.

"Gelatinous creatures. Spread out all over the place don't you know! Very difficult keeping the individuals sorted out. Had to use fire."

She looked back to him wanting to press on about what he meant by fire, but the doors were opening and they were in. Dehumidified air washed over them, the smell of stickers.

"Show me the list of things we're getting?"

"No, we will do one thing at a time."

This seemed like a serious point for him, but somber face made, he went back to happy. He reminded Bev of those actors with various masks, happy or sad. The actors would switch the masks instantly, or they had one mask with two sides that could be flipped in an instant. I'm happy. I'm sad. I'm terrible. I'm silly.

Wonder how many faces he had?

She walked ahead, into the main part of the store, hoping he'd come on along. Looking back, she saw he had pulled out one of those little flip notepads, Black leather cover. Probably had little lined sheets in there. Doodles. Did he make them? When?

He looked at it, then joined her.

"What's first, good old partner Mack?" she asked.

"Steel wool," he replied. He considered something briefly, then, "Metallic sheep, hmmm, not in my knowledge set. Then ethanol. And some kind of caustic agent, probably your glass cleaning solutions."

"Are we cleaning?" She walked him back towards housewares and this time he kept up. "Just tell me what we're cleaning and I'll show you the best things to do that."

"Steel wool, ethanol, caustic agent, preferably liquid," as if she'd said nothing.

She did not like being ignored. They reached household cleaning.

Instead of going to the items, it was her turn to stop in the middle of the aisle, wave her hand up and down the racks.

"Do you know what these things are? Any of these things? Have you ever been to any of these places, seen any of these products?"

"I have not, young Beverly. This is your place to shine! Now the wool of the metallic sheep please."

She went halfway down the aisle. She picked up a box of steel wool.

"Do you want me to get a basket? Many times. You asked. I've been here or places like it many times. How are we going to pay? You know we need to pay, right? You know, money?"

With his left hand he patted the side of his pants.

"Ah! Yes, of course!"

He reached in.

"I have some cloth we will need."

From his left pocket he pulled out a large wad of money wrapped in a rubber band. Had to be 10, 20 thousand dollars.

"Where'd that come from?" she pointed.

"I needed it. I have it. Why should you care?"

"Might want some of my own," and a getaway car, she thought, and a gun and…

"I doubt it. Ah! You are using humor again! Very good. We will need this."

He returned the money to his pocket. The serious look ran across his face again, then making the appearance it was forced to make, went to hide.

Something was off here. Was she insulting him?

Playfully, "Hey, I deserve a little respect, partner!" She elbowed him in what she hoped was a friendly manner. "I'm not trying to manipulate you. Mack, you're my trainer. I have questions. How else could I learn?"

"In the accepted way, of course! I've been trying to ignore your improprieties. It's muck-sokka-rai .." He paused for a second as if remembering. "You have a pitifully small number of limbs and input pathways. I believe you use shuari. Yes, that is best. Shuhari for these circumstances."

"Shuhari. That tells me something?"

"Well of course it does. Do you not know Japanese Martial Arts?"

"No."

He laughed, and Bev became deathly afraid he would continue laughing.

Instead he said, "Shu Ha Ri. This is the way we learn and master things. It is the path."

"Am I going to learn Karate?"

"You are quite the excellent sidekick. Keep this going! It means a lot to me to have such enjoyment. No. Shu – which means protect or obey. You learn fundamentals, proverbs, techniques, and heuristics. I give you rules. You follow them. Then there is Ha – detach or digress. Once you have mastered following the rules and why they exist, you may break with tradition, find new approaches. This seems to be the level you think you are, but you are mistaken. Finally there is Ri – leaving or transcending the rules. You know the rules, you know enough of why they exist. At Ri, you've reached the point where while the rules are still there for primitives, they no longer concern you. That is where I am. This is why I'm your teacher, Young Beverly. You are just Shu."

That was it.

"I'm an old lady, dickhead. Why do you keep calling me Young Beverly? You look about half my age. And you don't know fuck-all about what you're doing here, otherwise you wouldn't be asking me so much. We need a partnership to learn, not Chinese fortune cookies."

"Well, that is not funny at all." He crossed his arms and looked at her as if she were a used car he'd just brought home and found was a lemon.

"And I would like to know," she continued, "what in the hell is the goal…"

He touched her lightly with a finger.

Her mouth stopped working. She felt fine. She was able to move it. She was even able to open and close her mouth. But it did not work – the voice. No sounds could be brought forth. She stood in the middle of Walmart trying to make her mouth work and failing.

He sighed. "How awful it must be to only have four appendages. And really only two are useful for grasping. None of them are really appendages at all, if you ask me. Sad. You are the larger one, yet you are so very small."

"This thing," he continued, pointing to her mouth with just a bit of disgust, "this orifice? It's the only way you have of communicating?" He paused, but only for a second. "But my knowledge set tells me that the appendages and entire torso are also used, sort of a reptile brain ad hoc interpretive dance, I take. Perhaps you do know dance and are unaware of it."

He touched her again, as if pointing her out.

"…of this…" She stopped, began testing the mouth. "Cat. Dog. It. Out."

Words?

Her voice worked again. Seemed nothing had happened. He'd reversed it.

"Hey…Mack…" suddenly quite concerned at where they were headed. "No need to get all huffy."

"Something is wrong." His somber look had returned and remained. "Our partnership is in need of repair."

"With all due respect," she held her hands palm forward as if stopping a bus. She was desperately trying to remember any Japanese movie she'd ever watched, "old and revered Mack Azure. I am your humble partner willing to do whatever you'd like. There are times, great one, where I need to know things. I find that when I come to you with these mysteries in search of an answer, all I get is no answer, nonsense, silliness, or non-sequiturs. The fault must be mine."

She stopped. Please don't poke me again. Please don't touch me. Please don't get angry.

Worried about where he was going, she layered it on some more, hoping he had no idea what was appropriate or not. Perhaps he didn't care. "Maybe it would be better if you could assume that I'm correct from time to time. Not always, of course. It is a small thing. But I could be right now and then, right? You don't have to be well, such a little shit."

"Ha! More humor! Perhaps all is not lost." He thought for a second. He carefully placed one hand in the other, as if he were a professor giving a lecture. "You would like me to play pretend as if you know enough to ask questions. Very well. Ask me one of your questions, a training question."

Was this a trick?

"Ok, what do we need to buy all of these things for?"

Simple enough. This guy was like a brick. Maybe she could build something useful with him.

"Because we have a xenomorph shapeshifter on our training list to subdue. Ever done that? Would you know one even if you saw it?"

He looked about and she was instantly afraid a hairy spider would jump at her from the wet wipes.

"Don't fear," he continued. "You see all of this, this Walmart of shopping. As do I, by the way. But the USI is presenting things to you in this way, Young Beverly, because you have no frame of reference. There will be no underground burrowing brain suckers for us, at least not yet."

He seemed disappointed.

She went from being afraid of the shelves to being afraid of the floor.

"You see," he continued, "it's not that you don't know things. It's not as if you could ask simple questions, get simple answers, and be done with it. You don't even know what you don't know. That is, you don't even know the questions you should be asking, and engaging you in this way would only be an endless waste of time. We could spend the rest of the day mindlessly chatting about the origins and nature of xenomorphs, their rebellion and the time of the Dark Cloud. There are trillions of advanced cultures and we have much more important things to learn."

She went back to looking at him. Maybe he had a point.

"You find these amusing and silly, the things I say." He continued, "I also find many of your sayings and ideas silly! This relationship might be most enjoyable for both of us. But I do not seek to deceive you. When you go to one of your experts, your shamans, isn't it just as absurd? You ask your doctor about a cancer and he tells you it's the size of a melon. There are no melons in your body; cancers are nothing like melons, and melons don't even have one size. Why would he say such a silly thing? Because this is the thing you know, most of you primitives know: eating melons. You know very little, no matter what you think."

He held up the steel wool.

"Melons."

He went back to crossing his arms. He was considering something. She didn't want to know what.

"There is a good reason we pair off like this," he said. "Settle down. It'll all come to you, I promise, or I wouldn't be doing my job, don't you know!"

She shook her head no in response, even though she didn't want to.

"Are you telling me that I have no choice in even the questions I ask?"

"That's exactly right."

"That's unacceptable." She was in for it now.

He just shrugged, then he went around the store getting whatever was in his mind, as if he went to Walmarts every day of the week. He asked her nothing else.

She tagged along, both afraid to say anything and afraid not to say anything.

"We need to fix this, you're right, the relationship," she finally said as they finished checking out and headed towards the exit.

He didn't turn to her, but the automatic door did not open.

They both stood there, staring at it, neither one speaking. A man behind them went up to the sensor. He was an employee. He hit it.

The door opened.

"Must have been stuck," he offered to let them go first, then, seeing their refusal, said "Dumb door. Never done that before."

"You're going to have to let me participate more." She didn't dare look at him.

The air was dank. Rain was indeed on the way.

He touched her arm as they approached the crosswalk.

"Maybe you could do with one less appendage," in a flat voice.

Her left arm went completely numb. Horrified, she looked down at it. Yes, still there. No, not working.

"You seem not to need so many," he added as they crossed, still no inflection.

She shook her shoulder, the arm was there but not there.

He'd take her apart piece-by-piece, she realized. It'd be like pulling wings off a fly for him.

She thought back to Winkies. She'd pushed him to the point of killing her and he laughed it off, but he didn't. There might be something there. Hell, she had nothing to lose.

"This isn't going to work if you torture me, Mack," she said in the same flat voice he had, both of them walking to the car. "I'll resent it. Trust me. I've been in your shoes before."

He glanced at his shoes.

His naiveté was troubling, and at the same time, her own analogy chilled her just as much. She *had* been in his shoes. The idea that she was once him was insane. She was helping people, not introducing them to some crazy world of the afterlife. She had the normal world. Mack did not. He knotted like a brick in her belly.

They got to the car. Like a good gentleman, he actually went to the passenger door, opened it up, then looked at her.

"Will you agree to my way as long as I let you…" He tossed his hand around, not to be bothered. "…blabber on and on with the chit-chat, silly questions, and pointless talk? I will try to continue viewing it all as your small attempt at humor."

She nodded. She figured that was as good as it was going to get.

"Good. Good!" the smile returned. He looked down on her sitting,

"Then we are back to being partners and our partnership has been repaired. Another success for us!"

He went around, got in the driver's side, obviously pleased with things, soaking it in before they left. He inhaled deeply the smell of dog feces thick in the air.

She looked at her arm.

"What about my arm?"

He started the car.

"Ah, it'll wear off. Nothing is ever permanent, is it?"

Out of the windshield they watched the ambulance workers load a stretcher. The blanket was pulled over the body. It was the homeless man from earlier, the squeegee guy. The ambulance left without the lights on.

"I guess not, Mack." She frowned, watching it leave. "I guess not."

Somber and sullen, the joy sucked out of everything, she stared out the side window as they left.

With her right hand she rubbed her left shoulder, refused to look at him, and wished that somehow answers would appear from the window. She knew nothing, less than she'd ever known, even as a baby, but she found herself caring more than she ever had in life.

Mack's attitude fretted her in a way she'd never been fretted.

What new horror would he drag out of the ether next?

Diner Disaster

FOR SUCH A CRAZY DAY, Lem was thankful he didn't have any more thoughts that needed inoculating. He had troubles, though, plenty of troubles.

He sat, or rather slumped if he were honest, in the booth at the diner, glad he made it to the restroom and watching Sophie at the counter getting their dinner. She was almost ready to order, two back in line.

Sophie had thoughts that needed inoculating, he could feel it in his bones. There was a reason they were out in the middle of nowhere, camped out at a Hamburger Heaven, lost and almost shot to pieces.

There it was, more evil bad disturbing thoughts. He let them run through, though. He wasn't about to get angry with Sophie.

She reached the counter looking back to him. She gave him a thumbs-up and a questioning look. In reply, he responded with two enthusiastic thumbs-up. It was a bit of fake enthusiasm and energy. They both knew it was a lie. She was a good friend.

"This smells delicious," sitting down with two paper bags rolled up and handing him one.

"Telling me. Haven't had anything since breakfast," he said.

She pulled out her food and began eating. He looked at his unopened bag. His mouth watered.

"It would have been nice to have had a menu," he said, wondering what surprise awaited him in the bag, not wanting to be disappointed.

Through bites, while still chewing, "Two burgers, ketchup and mustard, heavy mustard," swallowing, wiping her mouth, smiling and pointing, "I know you, Mr. Lemuel Rickenbacker."

"That you do. Did you get …"

"Chocolate shake," she handed him a Styrofoam cup, straw already in place.

He smiled more than he wanted to and happily opened the bag. "I guess I really need to mix up my menu."

"That you do," she looked at the rest of her burger ready to be destroyed, glanced over it. "Be bold, Lem! Next time try cheese."

"Not going that far," but for some reason he was annoyed," Get me salt?"

"No."

He didn't even like salt. But salt was suddenly very important. He'd thought about it only for a second.

"Did you ask me?"

"No."

"Then I guess there was no way for you to know, was there?"

He was very hungry and he didn't want to eat and he felt like a little crybaby and he was right but he was very disappointed in himself because …

"You ok?" She had put the rest of her burger down, "I worry."

"I'm good," he tried smiling, picked up his wrapped burger, "You know me."

He didn't open the bag.

"Only too well."

Now was his turn to look chidingly over the top of his burger at her. "Want to tell me what kind of quest adventure you're on? 'Need to mix it up' or 'We're all reruns' isn't cutting it."

He tried to give her one of his caring counselor looks. It was honest.

"Can't say," she replied.

"Can't say or won't say?"

"I'm good," was her reply, then "You know me."

"Only too well."

He didn't open the bag. Instead, much to the protest of his stomach, he put it down. Something was already stuck in his craw that had to come out before he put anything else in there.

"Sophie, something's bothering you. We need to get it out and talk about it. I insist."

"You're the one keeping secrets, Lem. You haven't been right since you got in that truck. Don't bullshit a bullshitter."

Lemuel Rickenbacker didn't want to press his friend. He knew in his heart that somehow their relationship was at a crisis point and would never be the same, no matter what happened.

"I'll tell you mine if you tell me yours," he said.

He winked at her. He was shooting for a fake scummy pickup artist joke in order to break the ice. Instead he looked like he was developing a nervous twitch, a new one, the muscles not working as they should. Doubling down on this plan, he changed into trying to make a come-hither look, smiling knowingly and moving his eyebrows up and down.

She had one hand completely over her mouth. He could tell she was suppressing a laugh. In response he raised his eyebrows and kept them up. Winning.

"Keep that up, Lem," she said through her hand with serious eyes on him, "keep working on that?"

Eyebrows higher.

"It's never going to look like anything, Lem. I'm sorry. Maybe a black muppet." She put her face completely in both hands now, twitching a little bit herself as she didn't know how to respond. He knew that she knew he was joking, and he knew she wanted to laugh with him and not at him and was unable to sort it all out. Her kindness made him happy.

Merriment won, much against their desires, and both were laughing in a subdued manner. Now Lem couldn't eat because he was laughing.

They needed it, though. The day had been amazingly stressful.

Looking with fear at her, knowing they'd never stop laughing, perhaps even create a spectacle, he pulled himself together and sorted himself out.

Breathe.

They had work. The laugher stopped. It was good.

Sophie made her serious face also, did a pretty good at it, then pointed behind him and said, "Is that an anteater?"

He looked. Sure enough, a little creature made its way to the back of the eating area, shuffling along.

"Armadillo, not anteater."

"Who lets an armadillo into a restaurant?"

"I don't know, Sophie, maybe it's a pet. Could be one of those service animals."

"Armadillo?"

He shrugged.

They remained quiet, finishing their meal, Sophie finishing hers and Lem making it about halfway through before giving it up.

They were still not communicating. They were dancing around not talking, not really talking.

"Dessert would be nice," he said. "What do they have?"

"I don't remember."

"Then why don't you just order for me, like before. Do you know what I'd like?"

She frowned.

"No, Lem. You've never ordered dessert."

"Without a menu," he felt a deep nervousness. He was a piece of dirt circling in a cesspool around a dark drain in an even darker sink. "Or you walking back-and-forth a dozen times, we're kind of stuck here, aren't we?"

It was too subtle. Not knowing how to continue, they remained silent. He made it through another bite or two of his burger.

He could eat no more.

"How much do I owe you?"

She refused him. "Nothing."

"You're a good friend," he replied.

"Am I?"

He didn't know whether to continue, so he stayed silent. Lem felt like he was hiding, right there in front of his friend in the middle of life, hiding.

He could feel himself getting angry. He let it go.

He looked inside the bag. Another burger. Girding himself, he made himself eat the rest of the first burger.

After two bites, he said "Thank you."

It was her turn to say nothing. She simply smiled. It was a nice smile.

"I DIDN'T ORDER THIS!"

They looked back to the counter. There was a very large man in very rough-looking attire flexing his muscles while yelling at the small girl. The girl behind the counter was a quarter of his size. His face was red, his head almost popping.

She was very relaxed, even bored. "Did you check your receipt? What does your receipt say?"

The man looked like he might punch her. Instead, he looked in the bag, pulled out a piece of paper.

Lem and Sophia shared a knowing look.

The man shifted, mumbled, "dammit" loud enough for everybody to hear, and stormed off.

"Not a place you want to have customer complaints," Sophie observed, then sipped her shake a bit.

"Got that right."

He crossed his arms looking at her, disgusted in his own inability to bring things to a head. She noticed.

She ignored him, or tried to ignore him, for almost a minute. Patience for both of them was running out.

Finally she hit the table.

"I got a kid, Lem. Ok? I got a kid I can't see. Is that going to fucking do it for you? Give you something to go fix? Now will you leave me alone about it?"

Lem put his empty wrapper back in the bag with the still-untouched burger, rolled the top shut. All the while looking at her.

Then he stared at the bag. He had nothing. Looking back to her, he finally said, "Why didn't you say something, Sophia?"

She didn't continue unloading on him, and for that he was thankful.

"It was years ago," she said. "I was barely a teenager. I can never get Tyler back, and it's eating me alive, that's why. Talking doesn't bring a kid back."

He looked down at the table, tried to stare through it. Oh my god, he thought, this is pain. I am helping and I am hurting my friend. It was horrible to do the right thing, a terrible goodness.

"It's not about you, Sophie," he didn't want to look up. Somehow looking at her would make it stop, and it had to go on. "I'm deteriorating. I won't have this frisky lifestyle I currently enjoy much longer. I'm also hallucinating. I'm not here to fix you. I couldn't help you even if I wanted to."

"But you don't want to."

"Yes. No. Not like you think." Get it together, Lem. Keep the words in order.

"I don't think," and she sighed as if giving something up. Something painful. "I don't think we'll ever be boyfriend and girlfriend. That's not in the cards for us if that's what you want. Get rid of it."

"It's not. No way," but he felt his face flush, much against his will.

"Then what do you want?"

He was quite embarrassed. But he started this, and he was going to have to finish it.

"Look around you, Sophie," he looked left and right as if crossing a road then back to her, "We're all in a machine, many machines. And those machines keep cranking out little Tylers, little Sophias." he thought "Little Lemuels." he grimaced. "It leaves people broken. I want to stop that. Stop making more. To do that, we have to be honest. You. Me. Honesty and openness is all we've got."

He saw her grip her fist then make herself release it.

"I'll help you Lem, already said it. I'll help the kids back at the home. I'll do the best I can, even if I have to go somewhere else to do it," she paused, briefly realizing something didn't fit, then continued. "But no, I'm not going to go opening up this vein every time somebody comes to me with problems. That's not solving, helping. That's just feel-good."

She made a disgusted look.

"But you're not helping anybody holding back like that," he said. "That's why you're running away. You. Sophia Blackwell. You don't even know who you are, much less what you want."

Oh boy.

"You gonna toss out one of those little bumper-sticker sayings of yours, Lem, like 'know thyself'?"

"No." Sure, he'd almost said it, almost said those exact words, but not now, at least since she'd stopped him.

She knew him too well.

"How about 'knowing'?" he asked. "Can we agree on simply one word?"

She frowned. There was daylight. Lem went towards it.

"Can we agree that knowing is more important than anything else? For both of us? You want to know more about Tyler, whether you admit it or not, and I want to know more about my condition and options, whether I admit it or not. Can we just settle on 'knowing'?"

"What are you suggesting?"

"I'll help you find out about Tyler. We'll see what we can do. You help me find out about my condition. We'll see what we can do. We'll have a time limit, thirty days."

"And then it's over."

"Yes, Sophia. Then it's over."

"Excuse me."

They both looked over. To their surprise there was the truck driver, bag of burgers in his hand.

Everybody had burgers, Lem thought, but it sure didn't seem like no heaven. 'Hamburger Heaven' wasn't the best name.

The driver wasn't angry. Lem hated himself for wanting to run away from this man. The man was obviously doing his best to look sheepish.

"It was wrong of me," the driver said, then turned to formally address

Lemuel. "I'm very sorry, young man. I was being selfish, and it was wrong of me. Both of you still up for that ride home?"

Done talking to just Lem, the driver pivoted and went back to addressing them both.

Sophia smiled, took Lemuel's hand, and while looking at Lem asked, "Going to do this?"

"Absolutely," he replied without thinking.

He looked from her back to the driver.

"I feel better now."

"I'm happy you're feeling better, son," the man seemed quite chagrined. "Is it okay if we make one stop first? Only going to be a minute."

"Sure thing, can you help me get to the truck?"

Lem knew that asking for help would help assuage the man's guilt.

"Happy to help in any way I can! Should've locked that damned truck. I'll make this right for you."

The last thing he heard as they left was Sophie saying, "thirty days," then she went to pay the check.

Later Lem realized that the driver had lied; he had lied about many, many things.

Corncob Jim-Bob

LEM DEEPLY WISHED THEY'D BRING HIM A CORNCOB, but they didn't. He watched Sophie and the driver come back from the store, empty handed, and darkly accepted his new fear of metal people coming to eat him. Thinking of corncobs was the better option.

Jim-Bob's House of Corncobs was not what he expected, but corncobs gotta go somewhere, and Jim-Bob's was as good as anywhere else. It fascinated him.

The sign had the name of the store, and was hung with hooks on a small corner of a small strip mall simultaneously in the middle of everywhere and nowhere. Jim-Bob's was the kind of place easily overlooked. There was a cartoon corncob off to the right of the sign, waving with little cartoon hands, wearing a big cartoon smile. A cartoon bubble said "Aw shucks!" Another sign in the window promised a sale, ending today, on "Artisian AmerIndian Feed Corncobs, Buy One Get One Free!"

Sophie hadn't talked any more about Tyler or what happened. They both sat in the passenger seat on the way over while Sophie acted like a kid on a field trip. She asked about the driver's life and family, how he learned to drive, and begged to tag along to meet Jim-Bob.

She was the lucky one, happy. Lem was struggling. He'd work up the beginnings of a good mood, then glance at the mystery box, wonder if he should flip the switch on his own, and think about the moon, metal man. He'd think about what happened last time, what he saw, what he thought he saw.

The driver got in, pensively, as if reviewing whether he should have bought something or not. In a blink, Sophia was on his right.

"Lem, you wouldn't BELIEVE the things they can do with corncobs! They had a robot made out of corncobs that would follow you around and make popcorn on demand. They had a heated wall of corncobs with this butter sprayer which would grow new kernels and even season them! You could eat corn-on-the-cob right off the wall! They had …"

"I'm sure it's great, Sophie. I wanted to go. I needed the rest. Don't spoil the rest for me. Maybe we can come back," he said.

"Well of course you could!" The driver looked over, taken away from starting the truck. "Easy enough to find! Right off the highway. Jim-Bob's open most days."

"What's that?" Lem pointed to the box he'd been trying not to stare at.

"Use it in my business. Probably not something you should worry on," was the reply.

Sophia chided him. "Don't hassle the guy, Lem. We've troubled him enough. All of this is very complicated without us diving into every little detail."

Lem felt his bullshit meter going off, but the driver spoke first.

"That's right. Took me years to learn the engine, the drivetrain, get the CDL. The legal parts alone are a lot to learn."

And the box isn't one of the legal parts, Lem thought idly.

He stared at the box, but spoke to the driver.

"I guess there's a lot more to it than just driving."

"Right son! Lem, right? The most important part of truck driving, at least as an independent doing custom work," now the driver looked at the box, but quickly glanced away, "like I do, is network, keeping your word. Folks have to believe what you say, sometimes even trust you with their life and precious cargo. That's where you start from, then we can teach you the more technical parts."

The driver smiled at Sophia.

That wasn't working.

"Where you headed next?" Lem asked, now directing his attention to the man and giving up the box. "Who gets the cocaine?"

"Being honest and trustworthy doesn't mean dumping out everything you know. I could hurt people. I sincerely hope you keep quiet about my cargo. I should've emphasized that more. Cops don't care about the cocaine, got that covered, but I'm not completely sure who might care about the rest."

Rusty tricycles.

Lem glanced back at the little shop.

'You have our word," Sophie replied. As she considered what he'd said, "How can cocaine not be a big deal, but Jim-Bob's is? You scared the crap out of us!"

"Good. Okay, I can trust you that far. Illegal stuff, authorities and all that, that's all handled by some of my associates," was the response. He thought for a second about what could be said, "I make the hauling deals with my friends. They handle cargo protection. I just move things and keep my mouth shut about everything else."

"How can that work?" Now Sophie was biting in on the apple. "Don't you get stopped or checked out by somebody?"

He shrugged. "I was told never to worry. It seems to be true. I've been stopped several times. Seems to be true." He said it again and looked to Lem like a student who believed repeating his previous answer was preferable to admitting ignorance.

Worried about the wrong things and not worried about the right things, Lem observed, so he asked, "Why'd you come back for us?"

Lem thought to himself, I know what you said but why really?

The driver frowned again. Lem thought the man looked genuinely apologetic.

"Told you. I realized I was responsible."

"Isn't being in the truck just as bad," Lem asked, "as wherever you left us and us trying to make our way home? You said our chances weren't good no matter what."

"Yes, it's bad. I can't argue with you about that," the driver said, "but I realized that taking you home was the least bad of all of your options. I'm sorry, like I said."

"Why did Jim-Bob seem so mad at you?" Sophia interjected, "Just now." She pointed to the store they'd come from.

His frown deepened along with his mood.

"I'm getting a bit of a bad reputation, that's why."

"A bad reputation at smuggling?" Sophie responded, and with as much sarcasm as she could muster, "Oh dear."

"No, not at smuggling," the driver seemed to say that this point was important, "Other things."

"Things," Lem repeated, "and yet this ride is our best option."

The driver nodded a response, silent.

Lem reached up to turn the box on. He had to know.

The driver swatted Lem's arm down.

"No!"

He looked at them both as if Lem had started to blow up his truck.

Sophie seriously paid attention to the box for the first time.

"Oh, you've got a Hammer-Jammer! Haven't seen one of these in a while."

"You know what that is?" Lem looked at her.

"I've seen them. Some of the drivers kept gear at the school Tyler's at. I saw that in the stack. Looked neat."

"Ok," Lem turned on the driver, then, "What the heck is it?"

Before he could reply, four policemen came from around the corner 100 yards away, guns drawn, heading towards Jim-Bob's.

While the others were looking, Lem flipped the switch.

There was a brief flicker, as if there were a silent flash of lightning or a photo flash going off, then everything was the same.

No, Lem thought, it was most definitely not the same.

Where four policemen were approaching Jim-Bob's before, now only two were. There were two other figures, sure, and they even wore police clothes. They were about the same height, but they had scales, not skin, and a slimy head full of odd angles, not a normal head. Something that looked like a snake stuck three feet out of the tops of their heads and moved in the wind, sniffing.

"What in the living hell is that!" Sophie almost screamed.

The driver sighed. His shoulders slumped. He looked like a man just hearing that his beloved mother died.

"Looks like lizard people," the driver replied, as if he saw this every day.

The driver was not emotional, at least at first. Instead he reached up to the box and turned it off. He yanked out the power cord for good measure. Slowly he began looking like he'd just heard his mother had died.

Lizard people, Lem thought, the driver saw lizard people?

"You're going to have to explain this," Sophia said, and Lemuel began weeping.

Lem tried to hide it. His grief was waves, overwhelming.

Sophie put her hand on him. "Are you okay?"

He stopped. He wiped his eyes. After a brief surge, it went away.

"I'm okay. I'm happy. I might be better than I realized, not so sick."

"I don't think you guys should come back," the driver said, still emotionless, now looking back to the store, "You could risk it, sure."

He looked at them.

"But I wouldn't."

"We're going to need to know what this is," Sophie said, looking to Lem for support. "That looks dangerous."

Lem nodded, maintaining his composure. Waves of emotion kept rolling over him. He maintained.

The driver crossed his arms. He pushed himself back so hard in his seat it was if he wanted to break it. Finally he began.

"Was out of work. Don't know. Probably ten years back. Sure, I had thought about doing illegal things but that's not me."

He challenged them to argue. They continued listening.

"Found a truck, right out by the side of the old gravel road behind the dump. Didn't look like anything bad had happened, just empty. The truck ran, so I drove it back home."

Now his legs relaxed and the driver looked at the dashboard in memory, miles away.

"Thought about driving it. Wasn't going to steal it, but I had my CDL. Surely I could pick up just a week or two of work locally. Somebody would come for it. Beats being homeless. Maybe I could drop it off again myself somewhere. I didn't know. Then Skeeter came, and everything changed."

"I don't hear you explaining what this is," Sophie pointed at the box again.

"It causes hallucinations, best I can figure. At first? I was scared of even touching it. After the first time? Might make me crazy. Could be some kind of military gear. Stay away from it, that's what I thought."

"Then why use it at all, why keep it?" Lem couldn't help himself. "You've used it a few times since we got in, right?"

"Right."

The driver was quiet for a bit, then surrendered to the fact that he had to go on.

"I use it because it's useful. I don't know why, how to explain it."

"Why all this Plexis Seven nonsense, the gun, back there at the restaurant, all that gobbledygook?" Sophie asked.

"I use all those terms because the people I deal with use them. Seemed important to them. I figured you were just another one of these crazy people I'm working with. You scared me, hiding out like that."

He looked away.

"Yep, might want to stay away from Jim-Bob's" he said to himself.

"Well here we are, asshole," Sophie was also looking to see what happened at the store, "You've gotten us in deep, whether you wanted to or not. Now what?"

Two of the policemen went into the store. Lem couldn't remember if they had been the special policemen or not. The box was now off.

Special policemen.

The driver looked to them, still very sad.

"Look, I honestly don't know where the line is, where you can know too much. People I deal with, well we're all kinda skirting the rules, you know, so we don't poke around too much in anybody else's business. But walking around, knowing about things like this?"

He pointed to the House of Corncobs.

"Knowing about things like this?"

He pointed to the Scrambler.

"I know that I don't want to know, and I don't think you should know, either. That's why you were in danger no matter what as soon as I found you. Gives you too many questions, too many things to think about."

Reaching around, he plugged the power wire back in. He trusted them.

He pointed to the store while flipping the switch.

The flash, then the two cops outside transformed into one cop and one lizard cop.

"This messes with your mind too much. If you want to be a truck driver, a real one, take my word and don't get mixed up in any of this."

He flipped it off.

"One lizard, one human, same as before," Lem muttered.

"Wait," Sophie said, "How can we all see the same stuff? If it's some kind of weird tech that messes with your mind, ok, but how can different people have the same hallucination?"

"Probably not something you should know about," he said again, but Lem could tell his heart wasn't in it.

"You gave your word, you said you always keep your word. Your life depends on it, remember? We gave our word. Our life now depends on you explaining the rest of it. So explain."

Forced into a corner, the driver did not look defiant or beaten. He looked like a man unsure of himself.

"Yes, Sophie, that's the last piece of it. I couldn't explain how or why. The hell of the thing, and the real reason I didn't throw it away was that these visions turned out to be useful. Some things I'd see I knew to avoid.

Some things I began to learn I could trust. That's how I figured out the truck could fly. I experimented."

"The truck can fly?"

"I'll tell you later," Lem said, "So you're just poking around, trying to make a buck, not caring what you're hauling or why, ruining good people's lives with cocaine and sauna pants? Rusty tricycles?"

"That's right, Lemuel," he replied, "I made some good friends. Skeeter was the first. They helped me and told me things to do or say. Oh, I think we all knew that I was not in on the game, but in a way I think they were happy about that. I couldn't be forced to tell anybody things I didn't know, right?"

They heard shots from inside of Jim-Bob's. It sounded like popcorn beginning to pop, the first few eager kernels exploding into nothingness.

All three stared blankly at the store, too shocked in various ways to begin doing anything. It was like watching a man with a three-thousand-foot tidal wave approaching: too scared to stay, too scared to run.

For a few minutes nothing happened. The policemen talked on their radios. Lem realized that they should get moving.

"Now what?" he finally asked, not sure which of them he was asking.

"Now," the driver said, turning to them with a sad smile, "We go bowling."

Bowling With Skeeter

FOR SOME REASON, **L**EM THOUGHT that they had a long drive ahead. Maybe there'd be a scary chase, or scary driving, which he didn't want. He was content, no overjoyed, that he wasn't alone in his hallucinations. That was enough, no matter what happened next.

Didn't seem to be enough for the driver, however, and the drive was quick, slow, and only two minutes. They drove the long parking lot to the strip mall next door. There, on the end, taking up a huge amount of space, was "FAST LANES BOWLING." It had one of those animated neon signs of a bowling ball knocking down pins.

He didn't know how to bowl. He didn't want to bowl. Bowling wasn't for Lem.

He did know how to walk, though, mostly, and having caught his second wind, he easily kept up with his companions.

Making it across the lot, he resolved to be more open-minded. Sophie was acting like Lem was an old stick in the mud, getting into a rut, and that wasn't him at all. She didn't know.

He'd think of some new approach while they were bowling. He knew he would. Lem had faith.

He was wrong.

The first thing he noticed? It was loud. Second thing was the smell of sweat, Lysol, and stale beer. Third thing, it was a busy, noisy afternoon at Fast Lanes. It made him happy to see that there were no open lanes.

A man that looked out of place on the far wall. He looked like Steve Bucemi, Lem thought, that guy from the movie "Deep Impact". The man was thin, very poorly dressed, smoking, and holding court with a few other people, taking up a lane, not bowling.

That's where they were headed.

The driver went on ahead while Sophie slowed down with Lem as he went at his own pace.

"He told me they could help rescue Tyler," she whispered to him as they got a few yards inside.

"Rescue? Why would he need rescuing?" Lem stopped for a second, taking advantage of a brief respite, "How'd he end up getting taken away from you, anyway?"

She pointed down, "You've hurt yourself."

Indeed he had, probably falling out of that truck earlier.

It would hold. The blood, while running down his leg, had dried up and the wound had stopped bleeding. Yes, it might need a couple of stitches, but Lem thought one more scar wasn't going to hurt things much.

They continued on, Sophia choosing not to answer and Lem choosing not to ask. They heard an old-style phone ring as they finally made it to the chatting crowd. There were four or five people in the gaggle, all looking like they should have been thrown out of the bowling alley instead of running it.

"…Man could make a good corncob pipe," The man Lem assumed to be Skeeter said to the driver, then turned on him, "Did you see them? The pipes? A work, of art, I'm telling you, real art."

"I know, right?" the driver answered instead of Lem, "Got three at home."

The old style phone rang again.

"I would have liked a corncob pipe," Lem said. It was true, but he didn't know why he said it. Thoughts entered, telling him he should be more assured, assertive, determined.

Inoculated.

"Well heck Lem, you should have gotten out," the driver said.

Sophie looked to him, concerned. "Why didn't you ask me? I'd have gotten you one."

"That's fine," he was growing more and more uncomfortable with the attention. "I should have. You're absolutely right. Maybe there's a website."

"There's something going on down at Jim-Bob's," a man came from behind them that they hadn't noticed. He was tall, thin, wore a too-large army shirt over a dirty t-shirt, hair a bit unkempt. Lem thought the new man was the type of person most people overlooked. Lem's type of person.

"Some activity," he continued, then noticed Lem and Sophie.

"See anybody," Skeeter to at them both, narrowed his gaze a bit, then back to the newcomer, "any kind of people that look different?"

"Nyah boss, just locals."

Skeeter looked at the driver, then back to the new guy. Something was disappointing.

Again the phone rang.

"Go on back to the office," he told him. "I'll meet you in five."

Skeeter looked at the assembled crowd.

"Well? Would somebody please get the damned phone?"

A pale thin woman in the back scurried off, her hand over her mouth embarrassed at the lapse.

"Why don't I buy you some lunch?" The driver looked at Lem and Sophie. "They've got a nice bar here. You could grab a table."

The meaning was clear. You're in the wrong place.

Lately, it was the story of Lem's life.

More walking.

"We'll stay here," Lem searched around. Maybe sitting at the bar eating a snack wasn't such a bad idea.

"You two come along with me," Skeeter said, changing everybody's plans, then pointed to the driver, "You too."

It was another long walk back to the office. This time both the driver and Sophie waited on Lem without appearing to wait. He was pleased that he didn't draw more attention. He already felt like a schoolkid being called back to the principal's office.

Skeeter's office looked like he expected. There were dozens of bowling trophies, pictures on the wall. There was a wooden desk probably older than the ages of all of them combined. Aside from a few electrical items that were very low-key, the office would have looked the same in 1860, 1960, or 2060. The eternal small potatoes corporate throne room. Manager of nickels, master of none. Skeeter at the helm.

Lem began working his way to sit in one of the many scuffed wooden chairs.

"Don't," the driver held him back with his hand, and that was that. Don't sit? Wonder how long Lem could hold himself up? He'd find out.

Skeeter had been talking to the man from before; they had been huddled and looked up to them.

She didn't look at Lem. Instead, while still staring at Skeeter, said to Lem, "I killed my parents," Sophie said.

Only then did she look at him, then back to Skeeter, quickly, as if she were suggesting they both jump off a cliff.

Skeeter's eyebrow raised in curiosity, but instead of asking, he opened a drawer. The new guy stepped back afraid of what Skeeter might do.

Skeeter pulled out a very small thing in his palm. It was colorful. He looked down at it as if asking the new guy if he wanted one. Skeeter's eyes went back to the man, who had stepped back another foot or two. Skeeter smiled a wolf's smile.

Lem leaned forward. He couldn't see well. It was small and green. Maybe some candy?

Instead of popping it in his mouth, as Lem expected, Skeeter held the little item between his thumb and forefinger. He stuck it out, like it was a laser pointer or he was using it as an example of something. Skeeter pointed it at the man.

There it was, Lem thought. It was a gummy bear.

The reporting man from earlier looked as if he expected to be shot, and a door opened behind him. A large, large man grabbed the new guy from behind and held his arms, looking to his boss.

"Take him back, see what he knows. He may need cycling." Skeeter said to the large man.

"But boss," the man said, "I don't..." and he was squeezed hard enough to shut up while the larger man hauled him off.

"Cycling? He gets a bicycle to go cycling?" Sophie asked.

Skeeter glanced over at her.

"You're cute, kid. Whatever you do, stay that way."

He still held the thing pointed at the two men leaving.

What, Lem thought. Was it a gummy bear? It indeed was....small. It was blurry. Sure looked like a gummy bear. He couldn't make it out clearly.

Lem prayed a silent prayer that he would not seize again. Not being able to make out common items just a few feet away? This was a bad sign.

Taking advantage of Skeeter's perceived kindness, Sophie asked, "Mr. Skeeter, I have lost my child Tyler to the system. Could you help me get him back, please? We can pay."

We can? Lem didn't know where they'd get money to pay for the fuel for the truck driver, much less whatever this man might want.

Skeeter carefully examined Sophie's demeanor. After what seemed like forever, the searchlight of his attention turned to Lem. Finally the driver got the spotlight.

Lem fidgeted, out of fatigue, worry, and nervousness.

He looked up and saw one of the little project boxes like he had seen in the truck on the trophy shelf.

It was not on.

"We gonna use one of those little boxes?"

Skeeter's face looked like a storm cloud brewing up over top of them and ready to unleash hell. His face was red but Lem felt the infinite darkness behind the man's eyes.

Skeeter looked at the driver.

"You tell them?"

The driver spoke quickly, a nervous man caught by his wife at the local brothel.

"Kid turned it on, that's all." He pointed to his head. "Thing messes with your brain that's all. That's what I told them. That's all. Should have gotten rid of it. Yep, should have got rid of it that thing a long time ago."

Skeeter looked to Lem.

"You flip the switch on?"

Lem nodded, curious, "Several times."

"He's lying! Couldn't have been that many!" the driver started.

Skeeter pointed the gummy bear at the driver.

"You! Keep it low key!"

Skeeter made a head twitch and the side door opened again. Another large man stepped in with a question on his face.

Skeeter held his finger up to stop the man, pointing to the ceiling, as if Skeeter had only one point to make first.

The driver didn't wait.

"That's the way we were trained, right…when…"

"You shut up," Skeeter said quietly.

They all waited.

Skeeter continued, finger still held up to the ceiling, "before you mess things up worse than you have already."

And that was it. Skeeter's finger, which they all stared at, pointed left, then right, then back and forth again. Skeeter was not showing them the ceiling lights. Skeeter's finger was saying no. The driver was taken out much the same as the last guy.

As the door shut, there was yet more overwhelming silence. Lem found it most pleasant. He could feel Sophia's body language telling him she was not feeling the calm.

Finally Skeeter said, "You two. You wanna go or you wanna stay?" He gave up the ceiling and now pointed at his desk, as if they were going to go inside the desk.

"Stay," Lem replied.

He looked to Sophia. She was shocked, scared, mute, paralyzed. Lem feared nothing else would be coming from her, and he didn't know for how long.

"I'm curious." Skeeter gave up on Sophie and turned to him. "Why do you want to stay?"

Lem glanced to Sophie. No help there. Then he looked Skeeter directly in the eye. The man still held a gummy bear in one of his hands.

"Because I get the feeling you can settle this, one way or the other. Help me. Help her. Whatever needs settling. Get on with it."

Skeeter popped the gummy into his mouth, savored it.

Smiled.

Lem glanced again at the trophies, the box on top.

"You in the middle of this?"

Skeeter swallowed the treat. Lem didn't need to explain.

"What if I say yes? Does that scare you?"

"Not particularly."

Skeeter grinned sideways, the way a man might when coming up with an especially snarky comment.

From the other room they heard screaming. It was a muffled sound, but it was there.

"Good grief. I told them to be quiet, be discrete." He shook his head as if they were all in the same room and he was very disappointed. He began to get up.

"I am so sorry."

Lem thought that Lem might be selling church cookies and Skeeter, the kind bowling alley manager, just couldn't afford a second box. He was sorry. Good grief. Need to check on the kids.

Sophia exhaled. She did not speak.

Standing, Skeeter smiled warmly.

"I'll be right back."

Skeeter went out the second door.

Both of them stood, worried.

There was thumping, scraping, other odd noises. Lem's mind started to fill in the blanks of what might be happening, but he let it go.

Inoculated.

Once he was sure Skeeter was gone, he went around behind the desk, searching for things. What, he didn't know. Anything.

Maybe there were more gummy bears in the drawer. What was he going to do, eat them?

There was a slate PC. Lem doubted he could get in. How much time did he have? An old-fashioned landline. One of those metal birds that bobbed up and down drinking water continuously. On the wall behind the desk he saw a fire alarm. It was next to one of those maps that showed people how to evacuate burning buildings.

Last thing Lem wanted was to pull the alarm and then be caught hobbling across the lot. Then they'd both be in trouble plus guilty of embarrassing Skeeter. Somehow he knew the second thing was far worse than the first.

There was a charcoal sketch of a tree. Nice lines, he thought.

Think, Lem. Think!

He looked back down at the desk he was looming over. Maybe he could threaten people with a gummy bear, IF there were more gummy bears, and IF crazy was somehow catching, which it appeared it was. Maybe he could hand out gummy bears.

"Forget that," he said, reaching down, gummy bear plan crossed off.

He picked up the landline. He dialed 911. Laid the phone on the desk, line still connected. He heard the 911 operator come on, talking out of the little speaker.

In the other rooms more screaming, struggling, thumping.

Sophia Blackwell looked like a lost kid in the manager's office at a Walmart, afraid of whatever might come next, knowing she was going to be in serious trouble no matter what happened. Imagining the worst.

She caught herself a bit, enough to look at him.

"Stay?" then she frowned. "Here?"

He started around the desk.

"No, Sophia. Come on."

He took her hand gently.

"Let's go on one of your walks. I saw the back door coming in, also on the map."

He pointed to the fire evacuation map. She didn't look. Instead Sophia was continuing being the small child looking at the arriving policeman, come to issue out her punishment.

He led her hurriedly but assuredly out the back door, holding her hand, using it to guide her. He wasn't that fast of a walker, with the crutches and everything else, but she didn't seem to mind.

He went to the right. Later he wondered what would have happened if he had chosen to go left.

After a few minutes – much too soon! – He paused to rest. He certainly wasn't about to take her on a walk about town. That'd be a horribly bad idea even if he could manage it.

His life had changed, in one day, just like that.

Lemuel Rickenbacker had spent the better part of seven years worried about and helping people in life-or-death struggles.

"We need to find someplace to hide, at least until dark." he said.

Sitting in that office, he'd learned something. It came over him like a wave and washed him away.

He pointed up ahead to the left.

He was done with it. He'd never be afraid of violence or death ever again.

09

Clown Car

IT WAS A CLOWN. The thing that Mack drug out for Beverly next was a stupid clown and a stupid ice cream truck.

She'd fashioned an arm sling out of an old shirt she found in the back, and she kept silent as she futzed around with getting it on her still-numb arm.

They sat in the patrol car in silence. They were on the side of the road. It was the inner city. Mack had done this wild U-turn in the middle of the four-lane when he saw the ice cream truck speed by.

Nobody honked at a police car, of course, although it was a crazy maneuver and Beverly was surprised that they hadn't caused an accident. He'd turned the lights on right away, even hit the siren once, that fanatical grin never changing. Bev thought of a child playing a video game for the very first time after having fantasized about buying it for months.

And now they were here. Watching a clown get out of the ice cream truck they'd just pulled over.

She began searching her memory for cop shows. The problem was that Bev didn't like cop shows, even as a kid. Hopefully she knew enough to make it work. Mack certainly did.

"We will now instigate the traffic stop," he rolled his grip on the steering wheel like a kid trying to make the go cart ride last longer.

He looked at her.

"You will assist."

She nodded dutifully, hopefully meaningfully.

He accidentally had a small frown. The frown ran away like the last one. One face, another face. Flip, flip.

"You may speak," he let go of the steering wheel and waved his hands about the scene in front of them. "Occasionally, that is, not too much. I will indulge you as a good mentor would a pitiful childlike recruit."

Two urges battled. She was afraid to say anything, but now she was afraid not to as well. Maybe if she had two heads, she thought idly, it'd be easier.

He might do that to her: two heads.

"I will comply, Great One," she tried mimicking him. Maybe mimicking would help?

"Mack," she continued, "Most Masterful Trainer, if you want to do this like cop training, I'll do my best. I promise."

He sat back, twitched. Happy news received.

"You see? Our partnership IS repaired and we will go on to great success!"

"From the bottom of my heart, Masterful Mack Azure, I humbly will make this training my passion."

She wanted to throw up on his head. He didn't notice or didn't care.

He clapped his hands in joy.

Good?

"Shoo," he ordered.

"Shoo? I should leave?"

"Shu. You will follow the rules I give you."

"Ah, Shu. Shuhari. First I follow the rules. Then yes, Shu. I will Shu for you."

The ice cream truck was old, battered, the paint faded. She couldn't make out the words on the back, but as they spoke, a clown got out of the truck, music started playing, and he began setting up to sell ice cream.

On the side of the road? He was going to sell ice cream here? There was traffic. She scoped the surroundings. They were close to a large low-income housing project. Maybe the clown thought he'd make a few bucks selling ice cream while getting his speeding ticket.

She hated clowns. She hated that god-awful calliope circus music these festering cancerous trucks played. She hated the cheap ice cream. She hated the smell. She hated the traffic.

She daydreamed about an ice cream truck, perhaps this very one, in one of those giant car crushers they have at junkyards, slowly being made into a metal cube, music dying off and blood seeping out.

Ice cream melted.

Good.

That was for another time, she thought as they approached the man who had quickly finished his setup. He hadn't gone inside yet.

I have all of my permits," he stuck out some papers.

She didn't know what to do, so she hung back off to the right and a few steps behind Mack. She put her hands on her hips. Hopefully that would be authoritative enough. Seventy-year-old lady in civilian clothes with her hands on her hips. Right. Maybe the clown thought today was take-your-grandmother-to-work day.

But that's what she saw, right? What did Mack see?

She didn't know. He'd probably lie if she asked him, if he didn't tear off her other arm first.

Mack also stood with his hands on his hips. She had been mirroring him without knowing it. She thought again of how he looked like a boy scout, cop, movie theater usher, tall, thin, square. He would have been perfect as one of those South American dictators from times past. He was all bluster and military, ribbons and doodads adorning a carefully constructed cardboard image.

But that's what she saw, right? He was in fact a…

She shook it off. It was for later.

"Sorry, sir, we are going to need to take you downtown," he said. "We'll have to tow this to the warehouse."

"That's exactly right," she added, stepping forward. "Best if you come along peacefully."

She looked at Mack for support. He nodded, pleased, still keeping his eye on the clown.

Whew!

"What'd I do?" the clown asked. Mack looked a question at Bev while the clown continued, "Speed?"

She cleared her throat. It was open mic night at her own special the end-of-the-world hellscape. Beverly Castler was on.

"Improper parking," she appeared to examine everything carefully, "at the side of the roadway. These tire treads look old."

She looked to both of them. Mack was proud. The clown looked like he wanted to spit.

She continued, "and would this truck pass a health department check? I doubt it. Nope, Mack, this contrivance is obviously a public nuisance. We're going to have to confiscate it."

She hoped the warehouse had a car crusher. She could dream.

"It's very bad," Mack added. That man could not make a serious face, at least for very long.

The clown squinted at them both, as if seeing them for the first time off in the distance.

"Oh, I see how this is. You're trying to shake me down." Now he looked directly at Mack. "You're doing this to another Guardian?"

Guardian?

"Examples must be made," Mack replied, shrugged.

She heard yelling. Looking over her shoulder, the housing project wasn't that far away. There were dozens of high density units. It didn't look like a good place to live.

She could see some young men hanging around the fronts of the building. They all had that young-man gang posture. Some of them were yelling, not at her, but back into their buildings.

Kids started manifesting, happy little people fleeing out of sad hidden doors, doors in the shadows. Half-dressed. Excited. The ice cream truck music continued. It was louder. It called them.

They couldn't have been fifty yards away, and soon half-a-dozen of them were within earshot and who knows how many more, maybe a hundred, on the way.

Mack Azure stepped towards them. He waved his hands in the air as if telling an airplane not to land. The runway's not safe.

"Replacements! er, children!" he yelled, "There is no ice cream here! This man is a criminal!"

They stopped. They listened. The music continued, "Camptown Girls."

"Your parents are poor! They are on public assistance and are alcoholics! You should not be having treats! You live in crime-infested squalor and will die soon anyway! Run away!"

Whoa.

That did it. Bev watched as first they were heartbroken. As Mack continued waving at them, they changed their mind as a group, running and screaming back to their parents. She watched a small one in diapers, having only made it half-way, stand in bewilderment at the sudden reversal in fortunes before beginning screaming and crying, turning, changing direction, running after the crowd.

The men on the front stoop took notice. Bev saw a couple of windows open in the buildings.

Still looking at them run, she started, "You really should…"

She let the words hang. She covered her mouth. That was a close one.

She rubbed her numb arm. Shut up Bev!

A quick just-checking glance to Mack. Ouch! Mack paused long enough for her to know that he noticed, then, seeing the kids fleeing, turned and advanced on the clown.

"Hey asshole!"

From the clown, now back to looking at the apartments. Adults were coming over, cell phones already out and filming.

Oh shit, she thought.

The clown took his shot, tried to reason with Mack.

"The children want ice cream, Mack. Don't you care about the kids?"

Maybe he was fucking with Mack, deliberately provoking him.

Mack took a quick glance back.

"We will purchase them all ice cream later. It will be an impressive amount. Their families will forgive us."

They obviously knew each other. Maybe?

She reached into her memories.

"We're going to put you on ice," she said to the clown, pointing, trying to sound heroic, "downtown. There'll be cream later. Going to the Big House."

Bev got closer to the guy along with Mack. She tried to fake a swagger, act like a stupid TV cop. Couldn't she just take him off somewhere and quietly, politely break his fucking neck? Carve him up like a turkey? Was that too much to ask?

The clown looked back and forth between them, reassessing his situation.

"Ok, ok," he held his hands up, "I give up."

Good.

Mack stepped towards the cab and peeked in.

The clown continued, "I'll come along quietly!"

He was obviously trying to distract Mack, but Mack was having none of it. Mack saw something in the cab.

"Is that a Scrambler?" turning on the clown, "You've got a Scrambler? Somebody made a Scrambler! No wonder they sent me here!"

Here? Earth? Scrambler?

Sensing the momentum, Beverly grabbed the man while he wasn't looking.

"I've got him, partner!"

"Probably not."

The clown squirmed out of her grip. Beverly never trained in detaining people, wrestling around and such. She just lured them in and enjoyed torturing them and whacking them. Good grief, she wasn't like BTK with the fancy ropes, knots, and whatnot. She was an old lady. What a loser BTK was. Asshole.

"We need to train you, Beverly Castler," Mack said. "More."

She didn't answer. She was busy trying to grab his arms. They did something with the arms, right?

She was too old for this shit.

"HELP! HELP! DON'T KILL ME, FIVE-O!"

Clown was screaming his head off. Smart clown.

She looked back to the projects. Now there were a couple of dozen people, easy, all gathered around making a video of Mack the Cop. The cop was beating up the nice little ice cream clown who had done nothing. After he cursed at their kids. And the things he said? Viral. It was internet gold.

Mack drew his gun. He held it straight up, but Bev could tell he was looking for a target.

Bad.

"WAIT!" She yelled. "STOP!"

Something died inside her.

"What the hell, Mack?"

Now he turned on her, gun still in the air, and he was angry.

Very angry.

"We're supposed to yell dramatically," she continued, trying her best impersonation, "from time-to-time. It is the way." She thought for a second. "It is the Shu."

The clown looked at his shoe, perplexed.

"The shoe?"

Mack ignored him, nodded, suspicious.

She pointed at the crowd gathering.

"These people are gathering. There's going to be quite the scene."

He looked over to them, still not trusting her.

She could tell he was unhappy at her observation.

In the distance, a gunshot.

There was no reaction. A second shot. Yelling.

Mack holstered his gun and his normal attitude returned.

Mack, her partner and trainer, instantly changed.

He looked at the clown man, his enemy, the ice cream seller. Now they were old friends.

Mack placed his hand on the man's shoulder. Hail friend well met.

"You and I shall meet again." he said. "Some other day. Count on it."

"Count on it? I'm planning on it." The man began closing up shop.

The lack of any beatings happening, more shooting coming from the other end of the complex, and the upcoming disappearance of the ice cream caused several sighs and complaints. The crowd began dispersing.

"You. Me." Mack pointed at her. "In there, now."

He pointed to the car.

Looking over to the remaining group, Mack said, "Nothing to see here, folks. Move along."

Some did, some stayed, angry and determined.

"Your ice cream will return shortly."

Glares.

"There will be free ice cream for all."

"Hey, free ice cream," somebody said, and the last holdouts shambled off.

"You will explain yourself," he said as they both got in the car.

He had a neutral look, devoid of happiness, more troubling to Beverly than staring down a hungry Bengal Tiger. While she was naked. Covered in barbeque sauce.

"I'm doing what you asked me to do, Great Mack."

"Explain."

"We have technology called the internet."

"Of course," he made the hurry up motion, "I know all of that."

"The people were taking videos."

He thought. He shrugged.

"I guess. Yes, yes."

"It would have been all over the Internet, millions would have seen it. It would have been a riot."

Another pause. She wondered what things ran around in that head of his, wherever it was, however many heads he had.

"Oh! I see! I have overlooked this!"

"As your faithful and honorable partner," she continued, "I had to do this. It is expected."

"Indeed you must! Excellent!"

He sat back, obviously pleased, then turned to her.

"Very good. Now I will tell you the first rule of the Guardians: Never engage with large numbers of the natives. One or two is fine. And before you ask why, it creates too much work for the USI to handle. We do not, I think you call it, as Guardians, have that much clout with the undercode, not as much as others."

YES! YES YES YES YES! Her mind spun around. They were bad with crowds! Perhaps they even feared them.

She maintained stoic. Need to move him along off this topic before he thought it through more.

"Mack Azure," she said formally, "Perhaps this is a good spot for you to review our training mission and the things I should have learned."

Instead of the important thing I did learn, she thought.

"It is indeed, Young Beverly!" He flinched a bit as if remembering that she didn't like being called "Young Beverly."

But not that much.

"Did you notice anything about the flavors of ice cream?"

"No."

"Did you see what was going on with his nose?"

"No."

"How about the third child to arrive? Spot any differences there?"

"No."

"Ark smock oink stink a duck truck!" It sounded like he said, "You need to pay more attention to detail!"

His eyebrows raised.

"What *were* you observing, anyway?"

"An ice cream truck. A clown. A stop. A crowd. Video cameras. Sad kids."

She didn't know what else to add. Should she be writing down everything she saw?

"Hmmmph"

He crossed his arms, frowned a brief second. It was a temper tantrum, for sure. She thought she'd give him something else.

"What should I have seen?"

"I can't tell you."

"Why?"

Oh no! A voice yelled in her head. Not questioning him again! Not why! Not asking why, Bev!

He squirmed a little bit. She was extremely happy when he stopped squirming.

"Because I don't know."

Beverly nodded, serious and somber, as if this all made sense. Just don't touch me. She stayed quiet, looked again out the window for answers as the patrol car left the shoulder and went back to the four-lane road.

10

Quarry Queries

HAD TO HAPPEN, SHE THOUGHT LATER. Their relationship was too unstable and chaotic and needed sorting. Had to happen, and she was the one to do it.

It had been six hours already. Six hours under that tree, pine needles making her itch, fighting off ticks and mosquitoes, staring at that stupid freaking hole in the ground, full of rocks. Freaking six hours.

At first, Beverly wasn't about to say a damned thing. She'd just sit and suffer. Not that Mack seemed to notice. They were here to see if a priest came by the quarry.

But of course they were.

He sat Indian style, hands at his knees. His face was abnormally peaceful, as if he might break out in Transcendental Meditation at a moment's notice. It was if he wasn't there, as if he'd transcended their reality.

As the afternoon waned, he gave up his pose and went back to his jovial self, still taking no mind of the inconveniences but beginning to talk.

He told her stories of how he'd struggled to make it out of The Guardians and into management. He told her that each time he almost made it before some unexpected failure that he had no part in happened. But, no surprise here, he was not specific on details – the locations, the jobs, the mistakes. He simply spun stories.

She had no idea if any of it was true.

Bev was entertained, she was enamored, she was interested. He didn't want to talk details. So what. Bev maintained. Bev endured.

Finally, running out of steam, perhaps becoming frustrated himself about his vagueness, he began actually talking to her.

"You see?" He patted her on the knee. "With the clown? When we work together, there is nothing we cannot accomplish!"

"Hmmm. You've got to admit that there was a bit of…" she pondered, "*randomness* to what happened as well."

"Indeed there was! And you took a risk with your outburst. Look at you, already moving along. You are almost ready to learn the Second Rule of the Guardians."

She thought she could feel a throb in her numb arm. Was it getting better? Or was it phantom pain?

"Your student and beloved partner would like to ask you a question."

"Indeed, I suppose you must!" He cocked his head admiringly at her. She was a new car that he'd just purchased and was especially happy about. "I will provide you with a wondrous answer."

"Why were you asking me about the ice cream flavors, some kid, the clown's nose? I keep thinking back on it, trying in my own humble way to learn, of course, and I swear that there was nothing particular about any of it. What *should* I have noticed, O Great One?"

Again his head cocked to the side a bit, a dog working a problem, and his smile changed from being the dog to being the master, admiring a new trick.

"The reason I could not tell you, Young Beverly, is that it's the way of the USI. You see, we do not simply transition from one level to another. At times the USI throws oddball and weird stimuli at us to indicate that our behavior is approaching the edges. Not odd enough that others would be bothered, but odd enough that you would notice. It varies for each person, and the response varies as well. How you react is up to you. One person might ignore it or laugh. We want you, though, Young Beverly, to experience more of these things! These strange things are indications that you are pushing the boundaries, learning."

She sighed, "I didn't see them, but that doesn't make me totally useless, right? I'm trying. You can see that, right?"

"Yes! Yes you are. Thrashing about blindly like the pig in the night searching for the acorn will indeed help you." He paused, "we only need to understand and channel it appropriately."

"Thank you," she said, and she added in her mind but did not say it, "asshole."

It seemed like he was picking up what she was putting down, so she kept putting it down.

"Thrashing? So some degree of my ineptness might help me?"

"It might," he agreed, eager for her next trick.

She continued.

"We're by ourselves, Mack, out in the middle of nowhere. Could we do a time-out or something? I'm not sure of what I might do to offend you, yet I require more information."

"What do you mean?"

"I mean no more hurting me. I want a conversation with no repercussions. It will be like it never happened. No bad results for me. Ever."

"Okay."

"Okay? That's all? I want you to swear."

Mack stood up, formal, and lifted one knee off the ground, pointing it the sky as much as possible. He held his arms up as if calling forth rain.

"I, Mack Azure, swear on the Great Oonlga and his many elbows, proud may they wiggle, that we may talk for a while here and I will visit no harm upon you as a result."

She was doubtful.

"I said it," he insisted.

Let's give it a flyer, she thought.

"I'm finding your training performance a bit lacking, perhaps at times even poor and inadequate."

"What do you mean, Beverly?"

"You could do better."

"I thought this conversation was about you, not me! I am beyond reproach, as I always have been!"

Glare.

"You swore."

Sigh.

"Indeed I did. Please proceed. As they say, let me have it. Sock it to me. I abide."

She began but stopped, looking at him with uncertainty.

He said, "I must warn you, however, that I may weep or burst out suddenly in hives."

He almost looked ashamed.

"Anything I can do to help?"

"I also may explode in a raging inferno, thus ending our training, unfortunately. No need to put me out."

Unconsciously she stepped back.

"But rejoice!" he said. "I will give you plenty of warning. Perhaps even two minutes."

"How big is this, hmmm, inferno? That you could burst into?"

"It would be several square miles. I assume it would appear as one of your natural wildfires."

She couldn't make it miles away given two minutes' notice.

They both heard rustling, nearby, in the leaves, near, off to the back.

A squirrel.

A squirrel, had to be. A squirrel. A real one.

Doubt.

"As I understand, you feel as if you're already mentally perfect, and anything I might add as your partner would be a mistake."

"Yes. Of course yes. Goes without saying. I am your trainer."

Mack thought about his words, rephrasing, "Sadly you are small and insignificant. But I love you anyway."

"And yet, here you are, spending all this time, as you just told me, out in the hinterlands, and you still can't get promoted."

Sadness took root in anger.

"And you, Beverly," he continued, "you say you have this perfect inner flexibility. You think that you can manipulate and connive your way ahead of me, yet your learning capability is not much better than a piece of mud. Clown nose. Ice cream. Perhaps you need large signs. You flounder yet you don't see it. You seem able to convince yourself of almost anything. It's pathetic."

"As do you," she responded.

He nodded.

"Perhaps," he said, "but just perhaps! I say perhaps I am similar to you in order to continue being quite noble and fine. You are lucky."

"Mack," she said, "be honest. Did you really think things were going okay earlier today, with the clown, the crowd?"

"No," he admitted. "Your actions were needed. You did the right thing."

He suddenly looked left and right, as if they were under attack. Beverly couldn't see or hear anything.

"Be gone!" He yelled.

It didn't seem to be directed at Beverly. Mostly. Right? She ignored it and continued.

"You said that some degree of my ineptness might help me? Maybe this, this conversation, these long-winded ideas of mine, are just random things I must get out? Maybe it's my way?"

"I am quite pure and innocent," he agreed. "I am the overly-indulgent parent, mostly because of my good-natured, free-flowing happy nature. I will allow it here, right now. Do not worry. You had my word. I swore."

His face darkened.

"But I do not think, Beverly, that there is anything to accomplish with more of this interrogation."

They waited.

Finally Mack turned to her.

"Perhaps some of the questions we ask here," he said, "this randomness of yours as you put it, perhaps the questions have answers, but I fear that they're most unpleasant answers."

Maybe that was as close as she was going to get to him admitting error.

She nodded. The stillness of the shadowy forest continued. The sun drifted easily towards the horizon, done with the day and meandering back to its usual nighttime resting place.

She was losing the day.

"Fine Mack, I don't trust anybody. You got me. But do you really think my heart and motives are bad? Do you know how many children I have saved from poverty? How many programs I've started, me, nobody else, to help those who are poor, downtrodden? I've created methods, texts, and courses that they're STILL teaching, even after my most unpleasant convictions. Millions are better off. There are doctors saving lives, right this minute as we talk, because of the things I've done. I've received more rewards and accolades than I can count."

She paused.

"Before my convictions, of course. You keep saying I'm conniving and evil. You're perceiving only the outside, social result of my work with the actual value. I spent time, Mack, as a child, perfecting my inner self. I became perfect inside. There, I said it. I learned."

He didn't come back at her.

She continued, "I learned. And then? Then I began judging. I had to. I had responsibility. I learned like all good doctors to cut out the sick and diseased parts that would only pollute us and cause more pain than good. I made the world a fucking better place. My inner purity and moral flexibility allowed me to make the world a better, happier place. I did it in the ways that were required. It couldn't be done on its own, social perception be damned."

Screw you, she thought. You don't know me.

His eyebrows raised.

"Beverly, you're confusing your pathetic rationalizations with some sense of morals. Don't be embarrassed. It's quite common in the barely-sentient cultures but you really need to grow out of it. You don't see that you're actually one of the most inflexible, untrainable blobs of rotting meat that I've ever had the misfortune to work with. My superiors rate me as outstanding, I'll have you know. Thank you very much. There are, yes, a very few things I need to work on, but not in your wildest dreams are any that you could help me with."

He was still smiling. Goddamn, she thought, he sounded like he was madder than a hornet but the fucker was still smiling!

First looked around the forest, then back to her.

He continued.

"I'm going to enjoy myself in our work no matter what, no matter how difficult you make this. A happy and relaxed training environment makes for better training."

Bev rubbed her still numb left arm. Didn't feel happy.

He advanced towards her. She countered by advancing towards him.

They moved close, within striking distance. Mack could knock her down with just one punch, she concluded, if not killing her outright. If there was going to be a fight, it would be a very short one.

He grimaced.

"I am perfect. What happened with the clown man and the ice cream was an accidental boon for you. You should accept it as such. Cherish such good luck, Beverly Castler."

This guy was like talking to a statue. Fine, she'd get out her hammer and chisel.

Her statue needed some pieces adjusted. She gathered her strength.

"You are the most inept, inane, ignoramus slimeball of a trainer that I've ever seen. You walk around like a seven-year-old tourist, stupid fucking grin. The only thing worse than your complete and utter idiocy is your quite frightening ability to hurt people."

Now he came back.

"I MIGHT accept some degree of randomness helping you, but I completely laugh and scoff at any suggestion that you are the one to know what's good or bad. ha-HA! You don't even know what planet you're on right now! Your species hasn't left your own planet. You prefer to bicker amongst yourselves. You use your resources to make yourselves feel morally, socially, and physically better. But you're not actually growing, becoming better. Frankly it was an amazing coincidence of chance that you developed the appropriate superstitions. Even more lucky that you developed them within the proper geographic situations that allowed you to advance as far as you have."

She had some words, but before she could start he kept going.

"Your lifespans are pathetically small. You don't seem to be very good at increasing them, though millions have certainly tried, haven't they? No, whatever improvement there might be here with our training, that's up to me to figure out, not you savages. Go paint your face and climb a tree, make sacrifices to your sun god. Our training is here, right here. Or you can leave."

She knew what he meant. Leaving was both an option and not an option for her.

She heard the squirrel again, this time far off. It was simply random forest noises. Right.

"You said from accidental chaos I did the right thing," she said, "and you said it was needed. These are your words, not mine. And yet when I provide some chaos right in your face, right here, right now, even if it's mostly or completely wrong, you become this rock turd piece of dark ugliness to deal with. You become a real shit."

That shut him up, at least temporarily. She went for it. Hammer time.

"How about a little experiment, just you and me? Can you accept a little bit of chaos, of randomness, from us savages without it damaging your precious and quite fragile ego? Here's news: it's not enough for you to look good to your superiors, whoever they are, you need to look good to the primitives you train. If you can't manage it, at least try to watch, to learn. Shuhari? I've got a Shu for you, bub. More learning and less shouting at children and killing the ice cream man in front of an angry filming crowd. You have factual details about us, sure, but the complex social interactions – you're a moron. Maybe even untrainable."

That was it. He was sad. Time to pitch.

"In fact," she said, "you probably just need to shut the hell up and minimize anything you do. Whatever you try to do inside our social complexities, it looks like you're completely terrible at it."

A good fisherman knows to provide the bait, then be patient.

"My goodness! I am not enjoying this at all!" he said, then was quiet.

No duh.

She waited.

"Hmmm," he said, "some bit of random interactions might help, especially with these complexities," he waved his hand at her trivial ideas.

He let out a long breath.

"I think you are stupid," he finally concluded. "But this bouncing around with the protocols and the like such as with the clown? It may be part of, a very small part of, a bit of new value for me that you've stumbled onto. It would be like learning from the woodchucks how to gnaw on trees. The instincts of brutes can certainly be instructive, even if they're unaware of what they're doing. Perhaps I can step back and observe. Yes. I will observe your pathetic, narrow-banded ritualistic social dances."

He gestured a trade.

"In this way we can help each other out."

Bingo. Wiggle room.

They were directly in each other's faces, spittle flying out with every word, death and murder still on their breath.

With his gesture, as if coordinated, they both backed away.

Keeping that happy light of evil in his eyes, he said, "Well enough. We will do this. You will teach, or try to. I will accept some of your shuhari."

She relaxed. It was a wonderful feeling. She liked winning. It'd been too long.

"However," he continued once he saw her action, "Oonlga does not have elbows, however. Furthermore there is no priest we are waiting on, and I have been quite happy that you've been uncomfortable sitting here this long. I was under NO oath that I was obliged to follow. It is you that have been punked. The punking was upon you most severely."

They both continued standing, angry in their agreement, tense in their settlement. There was nothing to say, nothing to do, yet they both desperately wanted something. They were commuters waiting on a bus that was long gone.

It got freaking dark. Cold air began seeping in.

Freaking quarry.

She wasn't about to give him the pleasure of anything.

Finally he said, "Very well." He left through the trees heading back to their car.

She followed.

11

Dumpster Fire

THE DUMPSTER WAS NOT ON FIRE. There were no pedestrians ran down, splattered on the ground and still twitching. There were no riots, angry mobs, or bank robberies in progress. Nobody ran up screaming bloody murder as they arrived.

Disappointing.

For Beverly, in the end it turned out to be much worse.

"Shoplifters?" She asked, but not seeing anything to shoplift, or anybody to be a shoplifter. It was all just a behind-the-strip-mall parking lot.

"All we got was 'public disturbance'," Mack replied. "Get out. They usually come to us."

Bev was not good at milling about, but they got out of the cruiser and she tried it anyway. She failed. She wanted to go somewhere, do something.

"So are we meeting real criminals, or something else? Like you. Like us."

He shrugged.

There was a clank from the dumpster. The sound of metal-on-metal, a tiny little Geppetto making a tiny little Pinocchio, somewhere lost in the garbage.

"Nobody's here." It was a weak voice, not a child, but not an adult either.

Mack gestured to Beverly as if he were introducing her to the dumpster, as if saying, "See?"

Bev crossed her arms and waited. No more sounds came.

"Hmmph," she said after a minute. She went to the cruiser, popped open the trunk.

Mack's eyebrows raised.

Reaching inside, she pulled out a road flare, the old-fashioned kind that burned phosphorous. She walked back, lit the flare, then tossed it into the dumpster. She rubbed her hand on her shirt as if she'd just finished washing it. Job done.

"Still nobody?" she asked.

"An excellent decision," Mack said.

Didn't take but just a few seconds until the dumpster started making sounds as if a man with a bat were beating on it from inside. The tinkerer was angry. There was moaning and muffled alarm, calls of "Ouch!" and then a teenager appeared, head and shoulders, looking at them as if he also wondered why he was there, a dumpster-sized jack-in-the-box.

Rats off a sinking ship.

No, Bev corrected herself – not teens, maybe early twenties. Instead of climbing, though, he was shoved out through the door and fell onto the pavement. He had braces on his legs and crutches flew out the door after that and landed on top of him. Finally a young lady appeared and clamored out as fast as decorum would allow.

"If we didn't have a disturbance before, we've now established one," Mack said, obviously pleased with the turn of events and watching the newcomers collect themselves. "You have great potential, Beverly Castler. What would you do now?"

Bev made them introduce themselves, then asked, "Want to explain why you were hiding in a dumpster?"

"We know about the nest pod of the delta swarm! Klaxon Forty-Three!" Sophia, the girl blurted. What the hell? Drugs? This Lemuel chap just stared at them. He looked as if he were trying to drill holes through her with his eyes.

"You can't possibly know that!" Mack had stepped forward and was reaching for his gun. He began drawing it, as if gunning down civilians was the correct response to dumpster diving. Bev liked using fire better. Anonymous. Plus they didn't give her a gun. Yet. What the hell, Mack. That guy was determined to shoot the place up.

She held him back with her hand, wondering whether he would obey or not. He did, put his gun back, and from the corner of her eye she saw him relax some.

"Should have kept my mouth shut," he said. "I believe the appropriate wording is 'fuck'."

Lem didn't look at Mack, instead continuing his piercing stare at her.

"Going to give us a ticket? Or something?"

"Something, I'm afraid," Mack responded, and he sounded grim, reserved. This was also new.

Curiouser and curiouser, she thought.

"What has got into you, Mack? Again with the gun? Cursing?" She asked him but kept her stare on Lem. "Kid's right. Give them a ticket, give a lecture, take them out somewhere and have a bit of fun, but don't make a spectacle. Don't draw attention. Remember the rule."

He wanted to know what she would do? Fine. He was going to get it, good and hard.

They heard a pop and looked over. Smoke was beginning to come from the road flare inside the dumpster finding something else to burn.

A spectacle was coming. That had been her doing.

"A worse situation is arriving upon us!" Mack said, then shrugged, "My bad. Oh well. Things happen."

More smoke came out, not yet a full fire, but it wouldn't be long. Was there some kind of otherworldly fire department he was going to call now? What the hell would they do? Who the hell would firemen end up being?

Doubt.

She was going to ask, but was interrupted by a cell phone.

Mack pulled a phone from his pocket, just like that. What did Mack need a phone for?

He said only three words; it was the same word repeated, with a long pause between.

"Yes…yes…yes." He hung up.

Her mentor was obviously destroyed by something, some piece of news. He shook his head, put his phone away, and looked at them all sheepishly.

"The boss. I have received my first demerit. Or at least it could be. I'm sorry."

"Sorry about what?" Bev furrowed her brow, then gave up her staring contest with the scarred-ass little broken runt garbage. "The boss? He was watching?"

The disappointment on Mack's face lost a battle with a little twinkle, a bit of merriment. He came back to them.

"Boss? He, she, it, watching?" He actually smiled for a second, then stopped. "There are too many words that I don't have the time or patience to define them right now."

He looked at Sophia and Lem.

"Nor would I even if I did have the time."

Sheepish.

"Mistakes were made," Beverly tried her go-to version of blame avoidance. There was something interesting here for sure, but it needed to stay controlled. "What's it going to be? A ticket? A beating? Take them downtown, wherever that is? The warehouse? I can torture them if you want, just not here. You've been gone from here for a while. Trust me on this."

"You police?" The broken one asked, changing his opinion.

Mack considered Bev.

"We need more. It is still simply a glitch, not yet an incident. I can fix it. There may be hope."

Now the smoke was continuous. Wasn't going to be long before all sorts of people showed up, she thought.

Make up your mind, Mack.

"You guys just playing around, right?" Sophie said, "trying to scare us."

"He's an angel," Bev said, decision made, "or close enough. This guy right here? He's an angel."

She watched her partner carefully. He'd said nothing about telling people things. This might be another ding on his record. Fuck him. Move or be moved. The boss was watching, right? She liked that.

He looked about as if expecting somebody to leap out from the woods.

"That's not true," Lem said. "I know that's not true. He's just some cop."

She could see that the boy had doubts.

Mack's phone rang again.

"Yes," he hung up.

"Yes," he said again to the newcomers, decision made as well, putting the phone back. "It's true."

Mack looked like a man who'd finally picked a suit out for an upcoming wedding. It wasn't perfect, but he had what he had.

He stepped forward and pointed at Lem. Mack's eyes went to the sky as if he were remembering.

"Lemuel Rickenbacher. Early twenties. Disabled. Some criminal activity early on, some rehab, Spirit Foundations is a great place, not much social media but enough to leave a trail. You're a religious person and you secretly wish you could run your own home, or a series of homes, to help people like yourself." He looked up again. "But it turns out you're not confident enough. I could go on."

Now he pointed at Sophia. He looked up again briefly then returned his stare to her.

"Sophia Blackwell. Much tragedy in early life, good grades in school, bounced around. A lot of social drama. Terrible parents, sadly. Ooh, some nice secrets here. Shall I continue? Like to talk about Skyler?"

The frail black kid started to move, stopped, then started again, as if he couldn't make up his mind, as if his mind were vibrating and his body was trying to catch up.

"Are we dead?" He asked, finally controlling his twitching.

"Not that lucky," Bev replied, which just made the little punk more confused. Bev found it all annoying. She began to realize the tediousness that might be involved with her new job. Everyone they meet that hasn't made it out of the DIM levels were going to be drama queens – dumb drama queens. Her job. Counselor for the apoplectic.

"My big mouth," Mack said to Bev, "I do not wish a demerit. My record's spotless so far. I was due a review."

"Why not just end these people?" she replied. "Who cares? Couple kids. Easy."

He sighed.

"Because, they told me we need to take them somewhere."

"Prisoners?"

"Escorts?" He shrugged.

"Restrain them?"

"I do not know. I was simply told to put them on the list."

"Kill 'em, stick 'em the trunk? Come on, Mack. Were you specifically told that they had to be alive?"

"No, not actually, just take them, that's all. Good point, though. Easier that way. I don't think the boss would care one way or another. I don't think."

They heard a racket. It was the sound of tin cans dragging down a parking lot.

The boy, Lem, was hobbling off as fast as he could go. It was like watching a panicked turtle making his frantic escape from a recent back robbery, missing the money.

"Lemuel!" Sophie said, "Stop! This is stupid! You'll never make it. You can't outrun a person. Or a car. Lem!"

He didn't look back, instead making go as fast as he could. The kid was leaving at about the speed of a walk.

"They'll hurt you!" Sophie tried again.

Didn't stop, but he did yell back.

"Just kill me then!" And kept working it. Spunky little brat. Sounded out of breath. Hadn't gone fifty yards.

Maybe if they waited long enough he'd just fall over, Bev thought. A wistful smile. We should be so lucky.

For such a smart guy, Mack was proving to be a bit of a corporate suckup. Bev might could use that too.

"I'm restraining this one." Bev grabbed Sophia by the arm and took her to the back of the car. Sophie could have fought her and probably won if she did, but the fight was out. Bev had seen this before, many times.

"Cuff them?" She asked over the hood. She didn't have cuffs.

"I don't see why," Mack said, then, "restraints, that is."

Bev didn't either, and if she deleted them here there'd just be more of this hand-wringing, so she just stuck the girl in the back and shut the door. Now they were both watching Lem's escape: Mack from beside the dumpster and Bev from beside the car.

It was about as exciting as she expected. Turtles. She remembered running over a turtle with her car once. Made a cracking sound, like a large walnut.

Mack curled his finger, indicating come on, let's do this.

Neither one of them ran. They didn't have to. They just walked up to Lem, huffing and puffing and hobbling along, refusing to acknowledge them, willing himself to be invisible.

She gently grabbed one arm. Mack took the other. Lem stopped. He kept staring ahead.

"Lem, right? Name's Lem?" She put on her best grandmother voice, "Come on, son, let's get you to the car. We can tend to you and you'll both be okay. I promise."

He came with them, but he didn't slouch as the girl had. Instead, for a limp sack of bones the boy was defiant. He tried to square his shoulders as they went but failed. They mostly carried him. He pretended not to notice.

She got him in the back along with Sophie.

"You rest now," she patted him. Then she took his crutches. "Won't be needing these anytime soon."

She tossed them into the trunk along with the rest of the gear. No more escapes. Simple as that.

The cruiser left and the dumpster burned. Mack was in no hurry. No crowd was there to watch them leave.

Bev looked forward to the festivities to come. Perhaps the day was perking up.

12

Giftshop Giveaway

"WHAT KIND OF PERSON WOULD WANT A CHRISTMAS ORNAMENT with figurines of people pooping next to a tree? It's also a snow globe? What happens if you shake it?" Beverly asked the man behind the counter.

"They're edible. Definitely not a Christmas ornament, unless you're into that kind of thing," he replied, bored and not to be bothered. "We also have a nice selection of candied dioramas of spree killers over next to the beaver cheese."

He was a small man. He reminded Beverly of the little goblins that ran the bank in the Harry Potter movies, except he was slovenly. He was short, fat, scraggly-haired, and obnoxious.

They had pulled into a roadside attraction with the two kids still stuck in the back. In between shops advertising the "Biggest Ball of Twine in New Jersey" and the "Jersey Devil Wholesale Store" was this place. The sign out front read "Earth Trinkets!"

Getting out of the car, Mack stayed behind, leaning on the hood.

"Go do your thing," was her only instruction. "This man must leave. He cannot sell these things. They are forbidden. He knows it."

She could see why. The place was a veritable gift shop for the non-human tourist. T-Shirts said, "They went to Earth and all I got was this shirt", "Yellow Star Pre-Annihilation Tour 1713", "Earth: Came for the food, stayed for the water", "I saw the cloud, but it wasn't green", and others. It was everything a bunch of low-brow cheap-ass creatures from other planets would want in a gift shop. She wondered if a busload of retirement-aged twelve-legged insects might show up at any moment with their cameras.

"Beaver cheese?"

"Made with real beavers!" he pointed, "but something tells me you're not here for that."

"No," she agreed. "Nope. You can't be selling these items."

She looked in the glass case the register sat on.

"Are these real human brains?"

"Sure enough. Just got them this morning. Fresh. I have my own special sauce."

He tapped the glass case.

"The case is refrigerated. We use only natural preservatives."

"No. Just no. You need to shut this down, leave."

"Why? I had permission." He began sorting papers beside the register.

"Why would you do this?" She had to ask, "Didn't you think somebody would eventually come along?"

"Guy's gotta make a buck," he kept looking through the papers.

"You're not supposed to be here." Continuing to look around at all of the oddities, she said, "I'm supposed to make you leave, shut this place down."

He stopped his search, looked back to her. He smiled a tiny bit. "Training, huh?"

Didn't seem to Bev to make much of a difference, so she nodded.

He nodded, satisfied. "I remember my time."

He placed his hands down on the case. "You need to tell me exactly what I've done wrong. I'm entitled to that under the convention."

Bev looked at a rack of postcards, trying to appear like this didn't interest her. The postcards had pictures of very bland things: a rock, a dead snake, the moon, an old time sailing ship, two snails mating...

She couldn't bluster and bluff a guy who was obviously four steps ahead of her. So she went nice.

"I don't know," she admitted, "that's just what I was told. I'm the new guy."

He cocked his head to the side, not knowing what to do with her. She continued.

"I only know that you're not supposed to be here. I know I have to make you leave. I'm sorry."

There was a moment, a brief point in time where Beverly Castler didn't know if he was going to come across the table and eat her, claw her with a talon, scream, or something even stranger.

That didn't happen. The man simply nodded somewhat wistfully, and said, "Okay then. I'll do it. I'm done here."

This was worse than an attack. Compliance?

"What? Can you do that? Aren't we supposed to struggle, argue, something?"

"I'm doing what you ask." He smiled bigger, "And good luck in your training. You can do it. I know you can."

She got Mr. Rogers.

Fucker.

She left the store and meandered a bit on the way back to the car. Mack sat on the hood, arms crossed, out of earshot of Lem and Sophie.

"Well," he asked, "Did you offend him? That one was connected, or at least he used to be."

"No," she replied, "I was nice, honest. I can be nice and honest when I want to be."

She felt like somebody had taken her brain from her, made a copy, super-sized it, and stuck it in Mack's head, along with whatever else was already in there. Maybe her brain was back there in that display case. They were trying the new setup where she could lead and he would observe. Might be good to tread lightly for a while.

"I do not believe you can be nice," he replied, "or honest. At least for any length of time."

There's the old Mack.

"Screw you."

His permanent happiness had a hitch. It didn't last long.

"For a failure, perhaps we are indeed off to a good start," he said.

"A failure? Was I supposed to do something different? There was no public scene. He knew about the training. Was he like a Guardian gone bad? Should I have let him go?"

"Ha! Not at all!" He snickered. "You could not have survived any form of combat with him. He was not 'bad' as you say. He was simply pushing things where he wasn't supposed to."

"So it was okay for him to be here, but not running a store?"

"Of course it was okay," Mack replied. "What do you think happens to Guardians when they're finished with their mission, either flunking out or retiring?"

"Never really thought about it."

"Like everybody else, they find and create a new phase in their existence. Some pick a planet or colony and join up. Some get body modifications. There's always a few that hang out around the shop, attempting to add advice or help, usually just getting in the way. Tired of that, they eventually start causing small-scale trouble. I think you call this an 'attention-seeking device'? It's never so much to be very serious, but it's enough to bring back some of the old crew, The Guardians. We're quite lucky we didn't spend a long lunch telling one another glorious stories of our professional struggles and accomplishments. He knew what the game was. He has already spent a long time in our shoes."

Mack looked as if he would begin his own story. Instead, he pointed at her with three fingers.

"What have you learned, Beverly Castler, Junior Guardian and small-minded trainee?"

She thought for a moment.

"That people respect the job? I didn't know anything, yet he was assured enough about what I was doing for it not to matter."

"And yet I have learned nothing," Mack said.

"You were wanting more of the human social randomness where I can demonstrate opportunities for your learning."

"Woodchuck," he nodded.

She thought with that idiotic smile of his he nodded like somebody might when a child tells them an incredible story.

She looked at him, chewing it over.

"You're saying that everything we do has to be training both of us at the same time? I train you simultaneously with you training me?"

"That is what we agreed to."

"You can't come along, at least you can't interact. That would destroy my training. I need to think on this."

She absentmindedly felt her broach.

"Mack, you don't think this went well. What if I tell you what happened in more detail, maybe record it?"

"Your ability to communicate is so vastly inferior, we could be here hundreds of cycles around your local star. I am afraid, my partner, that I don't have the patience for that. I need to be there, even if silent."

There was silence as both worked through possible solutions. Almost simultaneously they turned to look at Lem and Sophie still in the back of the car.

An idea.

"Did they forbid us from using them on our way to drop them off?"

"They did not! An excellent idea. It is much better than killing and eating them. We will pair you up. Pick the one you like. I suggest you avoid the broken one as it would cause more trouble than it's worth."

She walked over to the back door. He stopped her before she opened it though.

"No more information for them though," his face was now murderous. He had the face of the forest argument elf again. "We can tell them our general job and a bit of what we do, but no details. Nothing they could document or take somewhere. We will get them discontinued and possibly ourselves discontinued as well if we continue unwise sharing."

She paused.

"Because we're here to protect the humans."

"ha HA!" he laughed again, "You, Beverly, are always good for a laugh! I admire you. No, no, nobody cares about these pathetic monkey-brains. Humans? We're not cops for the living. We're cops for the dead."

13

The Millers

"YOU CAN GO STRAIGHT TO HELL!" The man yelled at his partner.

"If only we could be so lucky," Bev observed, mostly to herself, before wading into the ongoing domestic abuse in the middle of the city park.

They didn't listen, too engaged with one another. Bev thought they made a fine group: a male-female couple madder than shit at one another, a small black boy named Lem who couldn't move, and a giant smiling tree called Mack Azure that refused to move. And Bev, the star. Mack was a smiling tree, taking it all in but reacting not in the least.

The girl, Sophia, stayed in the car. Bev thought the girl might take a while before she came back to the world. Mack had told her that they had a domestic disturbance in the nearby park and Beverly was supposed to calm it down.

Before they got out of the car, Bev asked Mack, "Are they, um, special?"

"I will offer you no advice," he replied, "only observe, as agreed."

"Great. I'll take the broken one," indicating Lem.

"Why? He will be troublesome. I suggested you take the other."

They both looked at Sophie.

That obviously wasn't going to work.

Now here they were, broad daylight, city park, and 62-year-old Beverly Castler supposed to calm these two lunatics down all the while looking like she was leading an oversized trick-or-treating group from the Twilight Zone.

"You need to break this up right now!" Bev yelled in her best cop voice, wondering if yelling at people who were already angry was a good idea. Maybe she should have a stick to beat them with?

But Lem had already gotten in the way, and as she watched he hobbled almost into the angry man. He placed himself directly between the two combatants.

The shouting stopped. Nobody was going to beat up a kid with crutches and braces. Lem touched the man kindly on the arm.

"Hey man, what's bothering you?"

Bev wanted to jump in and continue her shtick, but Lem obviously was front-and-center, and perhaps Bev could see the little crippled boy get beat up today. Beats dealing with the alien lugnut beside her.

"She spent the last of our money on those stupid spoons she collects, and we needed that for cat food!"

He pointed at the girl. She shook her fist at him.

"We don't have a cat, asshole!"

"He might come back! You don't know! It was your yelling…"

"Hey," Lem said, "hey, hey, hey. How much you need for the cat food?"

The man considered.

"I don't know. Fifty bucks maybe. She took a hundred, that witch. Our last hundred, and I don't get paid until Friday."

Lem looked back to Mack.

"We got a hundred bucks? Maybe two hundred?"

The tree of Mack moved, only slightly, and only enough to retrieve the requested money and hand it to Lem.

Lem leaned back towards the man, almost falling into him. Bev saw that the man was worried about him.

"This okay? This make it right?"

Lem handed him two hundred dollars.

The man sounded like an inflatable raft that had just been sliced with a sharp knife. All the anger left him.

"Yeah, I guess so."

But Lem wasn't done.

"Why don't you give her fifty, show her that you love her."

"If you think…" the man glared at her, then cut his eyes back to Lemuel. "Yeaaahhhhh." he strung it out. "I guess so. You're right."

As the man gave his partner the money, Lem put his hands on both of them using his armpits to hold the crutches.

"Now you're even. Don't you both feel better about it? What was the cat's name?"

"Beserko."

"How long he been gone?"

"Two weeks."

Lem pulled back, addressed only the man.

"You buy that food. He'll come back. I know it."

And that was that. Situation defused, the couple walked off, holding hands.

Beverly was frustrated beyond measure. She looked around. Maybe there was a litterer or a drunken bum she could hassle, but no luck.

Mack, Lem, and Bev started back towards the car.

"What did we learn?" he asked Bev before they reached the car.

"That guy likes his cat," she said. "I mean he really, really likes him."

"They were in pain. We helped them," Lem said to Mack.

Surprised, Mack turned briefly to Lem, then back to Bev.

"Did you notice anything unusual, weird, odd?"

She shook her head.

"No. Wished I did."

"The man's shoes were glowing," Lem said, "never saw anything like that before. Like neon sneakers. There was a penguin walking around the bus stop."

Lem looked unsure if he should have shared.

Now Mack was surprised. He backed up, took them both in, and clapped his hands together.

"Now that's interesting! Very interesting indeed!"

Mack looked at Bev, disappointed.

Lemuel shrugged it off, almost as if he didn't hear it. Instead he narrowed his eyes looking at Bev.

"Don't I know you from somewhere? I know I've seen your face."

She needed to watch that boy.

"I get that a lot," she said, hoping it wouldn't continue.

She knew the type. That Lemuel Rickenbacker was the type that'd look all weak and humble, then cut your throat in an instant. There was fire there, no matter how much he tried to hide it.

Lem reminded her of somebody too.

Herself.

14

Dimwit Discovery

BEVERLY NEVER SHOULD HAVE BEEN NICE TO THAT BOY, that Lemuel Rickenbacker. It was the start of a bad habit she was never able to give up.

It destroyed her.

Mack was out of the car, cleaning up. Bev took the chance to try to shut these two up.

"This is the afterlife. Listen very closely and follow my instructions."

She tried to address them in the backseat without twisting her back too much.

"Doesn't seem anything like I expected," Lem said, "you sure this is the afterlife?"

"Better believe it. Better get used to it. Better shut up and do as you're told. Be a good lad."

"Sophia," Lem said to his friend, "we're in a really bad way. The driver was right. These people are mean and bad."

"Mean and bad?" Beverly asked, "I'm a better person than you'll ever be."

The girl seemed upset.

"I'll have you know that Lem's been working at his job only three years," Sophie said, "and we've got the best statistics of anywhere in the state, probably the country: 100% of the kids get better."

"That's where I know you from," Lem looked shocked. "You're Beverly Castler, the Murdering Madame of Manchester. Our homes were managed by your foundation."

"One of them, yes. I had about a dozen foundations."

"You're one of the most evil people alive," he responded.

"Not any more. Look it. Dead. We're angels. We can't be bad." Beverly said.

"You? An angel?"

"Almost," she admitted. "Ok, it's more like angel in training."

"Like Clarence in 'It's a Wonderful Life'?" Sophia asked.

"More like whatever demon possessed that little girl in 'The Exorcist'" Lem still pulled away back into his seat, as if Bev might somehow grow horns and produce a pitchfork at any moment.

"Goodness gracious," she clutched her broach. "You children are so dramatic. It wasn't all that. I was framed. It was the governor that did all of those things."

"She had the only execution scheduled that nobody protested. The most anti-death penalty bishop came on TV and said that she should be fried in oil. After she was skinned alive."

"That's old news. The bishop, meh. He was the worst crossdresser. Like I'm interested in the moral judgments of a bunch of barely-intelligent small-minded do-gooders," Beverly said, "Bishop? I've got TV preachers, politicians, random people in the supermarket, the guy that cuts my hair, and most of social media to provide outrage. Outrage is cheap, especially for bishops. You're not going to be hitting on very much more insight than any of them are. You see what you want to see."

"You're going to hurt us," Lem replied, "and you're going to do it in terrible ways."

"I certainly hope so," she replied.

She thought for a moment before continuing.

"Ever see somebody you thought was dead? Like a really close person dies, somebody you love and respect, and then you're in the library or at a busy concert and across the crowd you could swear that's the person you just lost, looks just like them?"

"Yes."

"Exactly, we all have. Well, it was probably them. Welcome to the party, moron. Now sit still and shut up. We'll tell you when you can talk. Meanwhile, try to avoid the grownups' table."

"I don't like the party. I don't like any of it. While he's distracted, why not let us go? You don't want us here, do you?"

"No," she admitted. "You remind me of Forest Whitaker, that actor, in the movie 'Species'. You're always hobbling around with a semi-literate amazed look on your face. I expect a bit of spittle hanging from your lip."

"You remind me of Mary Poppins. Possessed by the devil. Sent by hell. Come to fix the children, one way or the other."

"Mary Poppins? Why don't you get a little closer? I've got some medicine for you."

Sophie looked to Lem.

"Maybe we shouldn't leave."

"What??"

"Don't you get tired of it all Lem? You're really good at what you do. At some point, don't you ever feel that it's time to move on? Maybe this is it; maybe this is where we move on to."

"No. That's an awful idea," he said. "Leave with her? With him? We'd be better off in the desert starving to death."

Bev leaned in a bit. He stopped leaning back and instead leaned towards her. He matched her.

"That can be arranged," Bev said.

Lem wasn't afraid of Beverly – not really, she realized. He was afraid of his imagination and what he imagined her to be.

She wasn't sure if that was better for her or not.

No worry. She'd figure it out. She always did.

15

Fish Tacos

L**EM DIDN'T LIKE TACOS.**

Sophia first mentioned suicide on the day Beverly went crazy and started insisting she could be a good person, she could choose, just like flipping a light switch. There was something in the tacos.

Something awful.

"Took forever," Sophie sat down at the picnic table with the other three, plate in hand. "There's too many for that one guy to cook for. He needs help."

"You could have just gotten a soda," Bev took a sip, "like us. Or nothing. It's a choice."

The lot and the park beside it were as idyllic and tranquil as a place could be sitting just off the four-lane. There were half-a-dozen food trucks, scattered about. They were advertising everything from "Frosty Fritters" to "Cajun Coondogs." Although the large lot was mostly gravel, it was surrounded by trees which began the park proper. Picnic tables sat at one end, neatly placed in a rectangular grid. People sat, trying to find the shade in the hot sun. The improvisational food court was adjacent to a city park.

There was a wolfpack of trucks and a litter of cars, maybe sixty people total. The food trucks were turning out a good business, and customers seemed happy to wait, either for food or for their phones to demand attention.

Sophie had returned, after what seemed an eternity, from "Telos Tacos," big paper plate in hand and stacked full of taco goodness, at least in her mind.

"You three should enjoy yourselves," Mack said, "while you have the time. There's a wonderful small brook over there. I managed to capture several images of your local star reflected in the murky polluted ripples."

"I'm very good just resting, thank you." Lem didn't think the brook would be interesting, not really, but Mack seemed to be quite enamored with whatever he ran into. Lem thought Mack Azure was a jukebox that only played happy songs.

Jukeboxes shouldn't do that.

"Soda good? Like it?" Sophie stopped munching for a second, studying him.

"I do, very much, thank you," he thought again that she was extremely nice taking care of him even when he was obviously far too much trouble.

Bev cut a quick glance at Sophia's tacos. "I might get some french fries," she rubbed her neck with her good arm. "I'm trying to limit my carbs. Tacos good? They look fabulous."

"hmm hmmm," Sophie had gone back to eating and wasn't about to stop just to use words. "Delicious," she said when she came up for air. "Fish tacos. My favorite."

"Is there hot sauce?" Bev seemed to enjoy asking Sophie questions when she couldn't answer.

Before she could respond, Lem came to the rescue. "Bev, can you just go get whatever you want, look around, make a choice, instead of asking Sophie to recite the menu of every truck here?"

As soon as it came out, Lem was sorry. "That was wrong. I've been a bit of a grump lately. It's not you. I apologize."

The older lady looked like she was going to take a bite out of Lem, but instead said, "What's wrong with you, anyway?" She indicated his braces and crutches.

"LBS from ABI," he said, then catching himself yet again, "Lower Body Spasicity from an Acquired Brain Injury."

He rattled a crutch as if that made the point.

"That means nothing to me." Bev looked at him as if he'd just insulted her somehow by explaining his condition.

"When I was very small," he explained, "I was in a car wreck and lost my parents. I hit my head which caused swelling, a slow bleed, and weakened arteries. My legs stopped working right."

She nodded a couple of times but didn't change her expression. He thought she was somehow sorting him, evaluating him, finding that he didn't measure up.

Instead of getting angry, however, she reached across the wooden table and lightly patted him, "that's such a shame. I assist several charities, one provides free prosthetics to children. We have some great cutting-edge carbon-fiber gear. I'm happy to help if I can."

Mack had picked up a sketchpad and had been working on a project but this stopped him. He looked over the top, raised an eyebrow.

"How'd you end up here, Lemuel Rickenbacker?" He asked. "In the dumpster. Behind the bowling alley. That event doesn't seem to be in my knowledge base."

"Smugglers. That's how it all started."

"Really?"

"Yes. Tricycles mostly. Sauna pants. There were a couple of sacks of dried corncobs." He tried to remember the list. It seemed like forever ago.

Lem thought for sure Mack would want to know more, but instead the man just nodded knowingly. He looked like he was debating whether or not to go back to his sketchpad.

Beverly shot a glance to Mack, "Aren't you going to ask them why tricycles? Why corncobs?"

"Not really," Mack replied, shrugged. "Why would I?"

"Because it makes no sense?" Looked like Mack was the one to get the wrath of Bev. Lem felt relieved, then felt guilty about being relieved. He probably started it all.

"Ok," Mack took the book down more, looked at him, "why tricycles?"

"Don't know." He didn't know. Hopefully that was okay.

Mack dropped his pad a bit more, pointed to Bev, "Happy?" shrugged, and went back to sketching.

"No I'm not happy. What's wrong with you?" Sure enough, Bev was getting more and more unhappy with Mack. "Does nothing surprise you? Or you just incurious about everything you run into? You're like a rock."

Finally the man put his pad entirely down. He surrendered, then went in a completely new direction.

"I had pets once. They wandered off. Curious and cute little critters. Couldn't keep them around, though. I had to get rid of them."

Once, Lem had a cat. It got sick. He felt badly. Lem said to him, "I'm very sorry about your pets."

"Thank you." Mack seemed happy enough with Lem, though, happy with everything in fact, as if he were done speaking.

Mack looked back to Bev, then to him, changing his mind and somehow deeming him worthy of continuing. But not her.

"I see you require more. Because of all of that, the neighbors? They had little pet babies. Turns out the pets were up to something! Little devils! So it all worked out. We got more pets. This time, though, I made sure they couldn't leave."

He made a chopping motion.

"A heartbreaking but inept story," Bev was not giving up her beef with Mack. "Maybe you can get a show on Animal Planet. Non-responsive. What's next? Show us their portrait? Sing a song about them? I was asking the boy here about what they were smuggling, not your pets."

It worked. Mack stopped looking at Lem and instead turned again to the older lady. But instead of getting angry like her, somehow he got more joyous.

"You have missed the point, young Beverly. These experiences are quite delicious! These are sentient creatures you're eating," he pointed at Sophia and her tacos. She was horrified at her meal, and suddenly had to decide between swallowing and spitting it all out. "Did you know that?"

The bites were too far gone to spit out. She looked both fearstruck and frightened as the food went down, whether she wanted it to or not.

"WHAT?" She yelled, finishing her battle with a swallow; the swallow had won.

Mack looked at Sophie the way a father might look at a toddler bathed from head to toe in a failed spaghetti lunch attempt. Amused.

"I will explain this to you, though I fear my explanation will be useless. Language using. Tool using. Abstract thought. Sometimes they get into the plumbing," he was responding to Sophia but Lem felt he was talking to the rest of them. "Hacking. Poking. Trying to manipulate the USI. The really smart and clever ones, as I understand it, are eaten by managers. Entire species. Absorbing knowledge and whatnot. The accidental and hapless ones? Individuals are given to the food trucks or whatever the cultural equivalent."

He winked at Sophie. Winked. Lem felt sick.

"Looks like the fish tacos you are eating. Are you still hungry?"

She pushed her paper plate away, but Lem noticed she wasn't disgusted. She had gone from horrified to contemplative, the way one might look at an opponent who had pushed all-in on a poker game, as if she wasn't about to let Mack get the best of her. She could meet him and fight on whatever his field of battle.

"This is a moral and spiritual nightmare," Lem said mostly to himself, but everybody heard.

"Spiritual," Bev replied, now switching to him, oops. "What an odd choice of words. What does anything spiritual or religious have to do with anything by now? Why keep framing everything good or evil? Don't you know better? You've learned. We've told you how things work. You're not ignorant anymore."

"I do know better. You're wrong." and for some reason Beverly thought that was the funniest thing in the world.

He saw the others at the tables look up, and for a brief moment he felt he had created a spectacle. But it was only another food truck pulling in. The placard read, "Smarty-Pants Ice Cream."

Smarty-pants. Sometimes they get in the plumbing.

He felt even sicker. His right leg twitched. He fought it.

"I need to help somehow," he said. Again to himself.

Sophie was staring at her unfinished tacos as if somehow they could save her lost child.

Mack thought for a second.

Lem found that the jukebox named Mack was now very calm. Somehow that made it worse.

"Would it bother you if I told you that I killed Tyler?"

Mack had yet to get back to work. Sophie looked as if she'd been poked with a cattle prod.

"Of course it would," Sophie said without hesitation. "How'd you know I was thinking about Tyler? How do you know Tyler?"

"Angel," Bev said to nobody, looking over her drink at the girl as she slurped it.

"Demon," Lem muttered.

Mack ignored the question but continued, "What if time passes differently here and they're already dead of natural causes? Would that bother you? What if I zoomed us forward in time?"

She was a bit confused but recovered quickly. "Sort of, I guess. I mean that's what people want, right? You get old, you die naturally. Never thought about time travel."

She looked at the sky then back to Mack.

"I don't know," she admitted. "Wouldn't like it, but I'd have to. It still hurts. But it's natural."

This seemed to please him.

"What if one of these other people killed him?" He gestured to the park they were in. "Say I pointed somebody out, told you he killed them. Would that bother you?"

"That wouldn't be natural," she blurted, then stopped.

She looked around briefly as if expecting somebody in the crowd to leap out, butcher knife in hand, then back to Mack, concluding, "Yes, we gotta fix that. If that happened, if somebody hurt Tyler, I'll have justice. We'd call some kind of interstellar police?"

He didn't answer. Instead he said, "Interesting. Very interesting. There's a line somewhere."

Lem pointed to Mack's pad on the table, this arguing wasn't helping anybody. "What are you drawing, Mack?"

"Fish. Might be good for tacos."

Mack held the pad up for them all to see, but it wasn't fish. It was a sketch of where they were, all of them sitting around the table. It was good enough it could have been a picture taken of Lem, Sophie, and Bev just a few minutes earlier. Sophie had a taco in her mouth, happy.

Lem liked it and decided to ignore the undercurrent. "That's very good. You have an eye for detail. Nice shading."

Mack put the paper back down, happy he'd shown it, and answered, "your injury was caused by a motor vehicle accident, correct?"

"Yes, when I was very small."

Beverly glanced again at the sketch on the table, then back to Mack. Lem thought she still looked hot.

"That's it? You going to say 'interesting' again? You're a one-trick pony."

Mack didn't look at Bev. Instead he cast his gaze back on his work, answering, "Interesting to me. Interesting to you or not," he shrugged. "Not my concern. That's up to you."

Bev pointed to the food line closest to them. "It's a shame we can't gain knowledge by eating some of these useless fellows taking up space." Looking back to Mack, making her point with her eyes, "Some of these people look quite yummy. I can find a knife. Or a club."

Mack smiled. He was being indulgent.

"Sophie, Bev has the belief that I'm being purposefully obtuse. Let us regroup, just ask me whatever you want, little one. I'll tell you whatever I know. Let's see if I can find you something that you'll find interesting as well."

"Great!" Sophie looked like a drowning person just catching a lifesaver.

"I have so many questions," she continued.

Bev held her hand up, stopping her. "Did he not tell you that he lies constantly? Mack's a fabulist. Can't trust him worth a damn."

Sophie looked betwixt the two, trying to find help.

"What?"

"It is true," Mack said, drawing the pinpoint attention of all three. "I do employ a lot of falsehoods as part of my work. There's that. But let's not quibble over details. You will be entertained. I promise. Young Sophia, I promise that I can make you say 'interesting' as I have done."

Somehow that phrasing bothered Lemuel.

Sophie turned on Bev. "How come you know so much, then? About all of this? About what's going on? You're one of us. You were just…"

She couldn't say the word.

"Executed?" Bev finished it.

"Yes."

"I died," the older lady smiled a tiny bit, "I suppose it was in the news. The media loves me."

"What was that like?" Sophie toyed with her plate. "Dying?"

"Surprisingly pleasant, actually. Smelled like pork roast."

Lem found his heart racing as if attacked, although he didn't know why. It confused him.

Seeing Sophie touch her plate, Beverly continued, "I'll eat that if you won't. I'm starving."

They were creatures. The tacos were people. Creatures who got too smart.

"Don't do it," Lem said. He was trying to calm himself. He was failing.

Sophia glanced at him, smiled a bit, then, of all things, pulled her plate back in. Carnivorous.

"Why not? They do it to us. Isn't that right?"

Mack nodded.

"And we don't feel it, do we?"

Another nod, then he said, "no."

Sophie pointed to her fish tacos. "Are they suffering?"

Mack had stopped smiling but began squinting a bit, as if Sophie were in the distance. "Not anymore."

"Then I'm eating them. They were tasty. I liked them. I like fish tacos."

She didn't start right away, and as Lem looked at her food, a fly landed on a taco.

He was simultaneously amazed and disgusted by Mack. Lem watched the fly searching, sprinting, flickering. A fly. What was the fly? What was anything?

He shook his head no, shaking off the conversation, shaking off the world.

"This is pointlessly confusing. It's pure evil. These two will keep us going in circles forever if we let them."

Uncertain, he looked at all of them, wanting somebody to help.

No help came, so Lem went it alone.

"If the system is evil, then it's our job to change it," he said. He pointed to the taco truck.

"Oh boy," Bev replied. Lem could see her working up some steam for a clever rebuttal. Mack, for his part, leaned in more. The squint increased. They were ships sailing off into the distance.

Lem continued. He pointed his thumb at the other two.

"Don't you see, Sophie? Life's full of folks like this. They don't have answers. They're not helping anybody, and they're not going to help Tyler. They just stir shit up. These folks may be nice, but all they are is entertainment, just like Mack said."

He gestured to Mack as the subject, but he meant everybody. Hopefully Mack knew that.

"Stir? You know how many people I've helped, Lem?" Beverly was incandescent. The serial killer was upset. Somewhere alarms started sounding in his brain. That seemed like a bad thing to do. "I have a passion for kids." Somewhere far away the alarm got louder. "I get letters every week, every week, Lemuel, saying how confused they are about my charges, how they always believed in me, and how I changed their lives for the better. Don't you listen to him, sweet Sophie, people can help one another. We all have it in us."

That was…this was…

Now he was getting very angry.

"But she's a serial killer," Lem looked at Sophie. He was desperate to help her but didn't know how. "She, the serial killer, sometimes does nice things. It doesn't work like that. Who cares? That doesn't matter. Life's supposed to be a struggle. You can't just give somebody a cookie and then hit them with a hammer."

"Did that once," Bev said. "You're right. It's difficult. You certainly can't get them to come back for another cookie."

It was Bev that continued, not Sophie, and she continued talking to Mack, not Lem.

"See that, Mack? These two want good guys and bad guys. Somebody's supposed to wear a white hat and somebody's supposed to wear a black hat. You want me to be the good guy, Lem?" Now she looked at him, "fine, I'll be the good guy. I'll wear your little white hat, ride your little white horse. It's not going to help Sophie, and it's not going to help me do my job better. Don't you get it? This life, this world, it's bigger than all of us. It's not just some piece in your moral religious cardboard cutout fantasies. We're not your cartoons. Grow up."

Sophie had found her life raft. "See, Lem? People change. Everybody can change, even if they have to die first. Bev died. She's different now, right? She's changed. We all have that ability."

It was weak tea.

Sophie looked again at her tacos.

Lem liked this even less. He didn't think for a second she was talking only about Beverly, and he wasn't about to ask. Life was crazy enough already.

"But why ask, if it's all lies? If it's all lies?" Once again he felt like he was referring to Mack but he wasn't. He hated arguing. He hated being here. Arguing wasn't helping anybody.

"Interesting," Mack said for the third time, and it made Lem's face go red.

"Will you stop saying that!" Lem heard himself say it; he made a fist, but it wasn't on purpose.

Bev's face was reddening as well, but she was continuing with Mack. Perhaps she thought they were tag-teaming him. If so, she was wrong.

"What do you care, Mack? So Sophie goes around making friends and tries to get help. Or she eats some fish tacos that turn out to be intelligent life. Is this our job? We going to sit around saying 'interesting' all day, or bounce off the walls like this crazed little guy?"

He looked askance at Bev.

"So, you want to be good," Lem said. "You know what good is."

Lem didn't believe it.

"I am good. I get to choose."

Mack crossed his arms, appraising all three. He looked like a man watching an unexpectedly funny TV show, about to change the channel but being pleasantly surprised at the last minute.

"This is the most fascinating you all have been since I've come back. Congratulations! Your language and sentience continues to grow and yet you creatures keep saying and doing the most amazingly contradictory things. It's interesting. I'm sorry to use that word again."

Lem glared at Bev.

"You can't just can't turn it all off like that, Bev. You are who you are." He'd never really wanted to hit anybody. Lem looked to Mack for approval and got none. Mack was still sitting, arms crossed, but now looking at the sketch he'd made, as if he'd forgotten some lines. A few details needed tweaking.

They had Lem completely turned around.

Beverly took Lem up on that. She pointed at him.

"You think I'm a psychopath? Well, hot shit, broken-ass kid, maybe I am. You don't think that psychopaths can be good? Being a psychopath is a lack of empathy, you little metal fuck, not a lack of goodness. Stop being so stupid. Read up. If anything, we can probably be the best of any of you. People like me are not encumbered by…weak irrationality."

"Hmmm," Mack said, not continuing but leaning in, wanting to hear this.

"Is that what you find interesting?" Sophie looked from her lunch to Mack then back again. "Bev's denial? She can't accept her nature? That she thinks she can change?"

"No," he waved his hand at Bev as if she were another fly on another taco. "It's your relationship to agency as you socially interact." Seeing they didn't understand, "It didn't seem like what happened to Tyler was as important to you, Sophia Blackwell, as knowing about it. Bad things happen that doesn't involve pointing at a person? These things happen. If I point at a person and say they contributed to a natural death for Tyler, again you're not upset. But if I were to add that a natural death consisted of writhing in pain from cancer? Now we're back to justice again. Even cancer is natural. You completely change."

"Well, if you're just making things up…" she began, but Mack cut her off.

"Watching you, the more information you have, the less happy you are, perhaps even angry, especially if there's some person doing something you don't like, somebody you can point to. Yet listening to you, you continue to believe and speak as if asking around and gathering even more information will make you happy. But that's not what you actually want, right?

You can see that? You want a gift, a gift from some person or creature with power over things; you actually don't want to know anything. You want magic, not knowledge. Knowledge would only hurt you more."

"Sophie, please," Lem wanted to hug her. "This is chaos, nihilism. He'll turn you round and around. I've seen it. Look at me. Sure, learn, ask questions, follow your heart. But to what end? Have a point, a noble purpose, that's it. Ends can't come from inside of you. That's the thing. They can only come from an outward-looking and humble desire to do good. You struggle with goodness, struggle with this life, gives gifts to others. Without this, it's all nothing. You'll become like Bev. Everybody needs a higher power. Everything needs a boundary."

"And I'll get them. I'll get a higher power," she said, "no matter what it takes," and that was the end of it.

Sophia returned to eating. She didn't smile. She looked away angry, determined, forcing the food in, forcing herself to swallow.

Lemuel Rickenbacker stared at his soda, not knowing what was in it and not wanting to know.

He decided it was root beer. His decision made him happy, at least for a while.

16

The Brook

EVENTUALLY LEM WANDERED OFF, saying he wanted to see the brook Mack was talking about. Eventually Sophia said she should go after him. Eventually Beverly said no, she'd go.

Eventually, Beverly found him.

She needed to come to some kind of truce with this kid, get him to quiet down a bit, otherwise he'd ruin her work with Mack. He was noise. Too much of it.

Damn if he wasn't down there comforting some *other* kid.

"You tell your parents that mistakes happen. You're sorry."

Kid ran off, smiling.

"Lem I want to apologize myself. I was a bit rough back there."

He came up, noticed her. Took her in. Dusted himself.

"You want me to accept your apology so that I won't be such an obstacle to you. Okay. Apology accepted. Now I owe you one."

"An apology?"

"I got turned around a bit. I shouldn't have let that happen to myself. I apologize."

Didn't that just beat everything to hell. Little bastard was turning her apology into his own apology.

She thought she'd make another go at him.

"Look it, I'm a cynic. I admit it. In my opinion, people that know, do. People that don't know, teach. People who can't do either, moralize. It requires nothing more than the ability to make yourself angry, then rationalize why being angry is correct. I can get that from my Dry Cleaner's. I don't know what's going on, okay? It makes me angry. I know better. I was upset. I was taking cheap shots."

She'd apologize by telling him what was wrong with him. Take that, punk.

"I understand you, I honestly do," he said. "We're all like that. Don't assume that you're no more or less broken than the rest of us."

Who was this, Ghandi?

She couldn't tell if she was winning or losing this suck-up contest. She went forward. Screw him. He was dealing with the master. Now you're out of the little leagues.

"For the first time in my life," Beverly said, "I'm having to work with and make important decisions using incomplete, bad, misleading information. I honestly don't know what's what."

"I get it. That's the life we all lead," Lem replied. "It's called being human. We're all children in service of some lesser god."

"If that's so, I sure would like to meet him. I've got some complaining to do."

"Me too. What did you mean when you called us 'dim'? I felt that there was some other meaning there."

"Angel stuff," she dismissed him, then changed her mind. This might get her what she wanted.

"Mack said we're not supposed to talk about it, but I'll tell you this much. It's D-I-M. It's an acronym for Death, Impact, and Meaning. Your meaning, your death, your impact on others. Any or all of these must be extremely good or bad to make it out of the DIM levels," Bev explained. "You and Sophia are still in the DIM levels. I'm not, but I used to be. That's why I'm here. It's some kind of math thing, like an opinion survey."

"Here?" Lem asked, "But you're not anywhere. You didn't go anywhere."

"That's it. Nobody ever goes anywhere. There's nowhere to go. Think of it as being one of those overhead projectors." Bev began. "You ever see one of those old-timey projectors where you have the clear overlays you can stack on top of one another? We've got one called the USI. Each transparency may have a different shape or meaning. You can combine them to make things you couldn't see otherwise, even completely change the scene, simply by moving around overlays. That's the universe."

"But you haven't gone anywhere," he still protested.

"But I have. And I haven't," motherfucker if she wasn't sounding just like Mack, back in the bar. "You're on one overlay, call it the DIM overlay or the default. Everything is all as you have experienced it and will continue to be logical and make sense. I've moved on. To what, I don't know. I've changed overlays. They've simply left me on the projector along with your default DIM overlay until I can learn to work with multiple overlays, I think. You look through a window and see you and I as part of the same scene, but I'm on a different piece of glass. So are you. So's the scene. There is no scene to look at. It's all overlays."

"Okay," he said, "I get it."

"You do? How can you get it? Doesn't that bother you?"

"Not particularly. Why would it? The math might bother me. Never good at math."

"I played with a computer at Walmart a while back. Best I can tell, it's all one-in-a-million. Mack said it's"four to the tenth and you're spent," 1 in 4^10, or about one-in-a-million to make it out of one of the DIM categories. So if a million people die today, it's likely that one of them will "win the lottery" so to speak, and graduate out of the DIM levels. Out of five billion people alive, there's probably five thousand that'll eventually graduate once they move on. To hit all three DIM categories is ridiculously unlikely but still possible because the universe is so big. It's something like one in a quintillion, one with 18 zeros after it. Assuming a trillion species, each with a billion entities, there's only a handful each year in the universe that make it into management."

"Management? Universe?"

She shrugged. That's all she had.

He didn't seem fazed at all.

"Great. Let's head back. Now I know who I need to talk to."

17

Glowing People

SOPHIA SHOULD HAVE NEVER SHOWN MACK HER CALLIGRAPHY, Lem should have never mentioned glowing people, and Mack would have been better off retiring.

Bev realized all of that later, after it was too late.

Things had calmed down when they returned. Sophia had a notebook out and Mack was standing, looking over her shoulder at her work.

"That is amazing, young Sophia!" He said, "Have you been doing calligraphy very long?"

"Motherfucker," Beverly mumbled under her breath. "Calligraphy."

"For years, Mr. Azure," Sophia was basking in the splendor of everything Mack.

Bev wanted to throw up. She couldn't leave these little peons alone for a minute.

"Might you teach me one day?"

"I'd be happy to!" she replied.

"I see you've made a friend," Bev said to Mack, "with all your lookups and whatnot, couldn't you have learned calligraphy years ago? Or river dancing? What do you need us for?"

"Oh, I wish it were so!" He stepped back, addressing them all. "Art is, let's say, difficult to learn without mentorship. I didn't find value in it and I should have. Of course, I could tell myself that in the past right now, but then I wouldn't be me today, would I?"

"You can go to the past," Sophia seemed even more enthralled. "You mentioned time travel?"

"A trivial thing," he said, "But the bifurcation effects are quite annoying."

"Ok, let's go," Bev said.

"As I have been saying for many years," Mack was giving a speech, to whom she had no idea, "Observing something today cannot change events in the past! This idea of observer-dependent retrocausality is not something…"

"Snail," she said.

"Snail?"

"Maybe it's like a snail. Different parts keep looping back on themselves but not the entire ocean. Lots of snails in the ocean."

"I hadn't thought of that."

"Also, you told me to tell you to shut up if you start going on about observer-dependent retrocausality. Now's the time to shut up! There, I've told you."

I enjoyed telling you.

"Is that how you get the glowing people?" Lem asked. "Overlapping timelines?"

"Glowing people, young Lem? Where? I have not seen them."

"Didn't you see the delivery guy, the guy bringing in supplies when we got here? Didn't you see the glowing person come in with him?"

The silence was uncomfortable.

"It was probably just me. Could have been an illusion," Lem said.

Mack was more enthusiastic than ever.

"This is quite amazingly incredible!" he said. "Vastly preposterous! This has never happened to me before!"

"We're going to need to go to the river," he said. "There's equipment we need. What a banner day it is. Now I understand why they were next on the list."

Now they all looked at Mack.

"Sophia. Beverly," he said, "I have more work for you two to do."

Bev noticed he spoke to her and Sophia but he wasn't looking at her.

He was looking at Lem.

18

Intercept

"**Stick with me, Sophie, and this'll be a piece of cake.**" Bev didn't look at her, instead they both strode purposefully forward.

"We get these people to leave, we drive away in their RV. Simple."

The Winnebago sat beside a large river. The campsite overlooked a beautiful floodplain. It, or some other RV, had been in that spot for a while. There was a picnic table, plastic chairs. A folding card table sat under an awning. On the table was a candle and lantern, some knitting supplies. This place was lived in, Bev thought.

There was a well-worn path from the seating area to the river a hundred yards or so below.

"So you've done this before?" Sophie asked as they got near enough to hear people moving around inside.

"Many times. Just play along and follow my lead," Bev replied.

She'd never done this before.

A handmade wooden sign next to the door said "The Grimes."

"We're cops," Bev said under her breath. "Look serious."

She knocked on the flimsy metal door.

Nothing happened, so she knocked again. There was some stirring; a man in his eighties appeared.

"Mister and Mrs. Grimes?" Bev asked, seeing the lady behind him. "I'm agent Castler and this is agent Blackwell. Can we have a word with you?"

"Susan!" He yelled even though she was right behind him. "Some official people here!"

Bev and Sophie waited the five minutes it took the two older people to come out of the door and offer them seats. Bev didn't think arguing with their hospitality would be fruitful so they sat. She saw the car with Lem and Mack along the side of the road fifty yards out.

"Sir, ma'am, we really don't have much time. There's a chemical leak in your area. We need you to evacuate, right now. You don't have but a few minutes, maybe an hour."

"Aren't you a little young to be an agent, dear?" The older lady peered over her glasses at Sophia.

"Agent in training, ma'am," Sophie replied. She sounded quite official. "I'm interning this summer."

Sophia was going to do very well.

"These two are with the government, Susan," the man said to his wife even though he'd already said that.

"Can I get you two some tea? It's been so hot lately." Mrs. Grimes asked.

Beverly felt her mood darken.

Behind them, they heard a car door shut. Bev turned and saw Mack getting out, staring at them over the hood. There was trouble.

"That's my supervisor," she continued improvising. "We're all training and we're in quite a bit of a hurry. Danger."

She shouldn't have sat, she realized too late. She was inviting more dicking around with these two.

"Is there some sort of trouble?" The lady asked.

"From the government!" The man said again. He didn't seem to care who he was saying it to. Perhaps the river.

"We'll have to insist that you both leave, right away." Bev stood. "Its important. Just leave all of your things right here. We'll move them for you."

She placed her hands palm-down on the table, leaned forward as if these two were criminals.

"This is for your safety."

"Well we can't do that."

"Do what?"

"Leave."

"Why?"

"Don't have a car, silly," the lady said. She was kind. "Couldn't if we wanted to. Can't drive this and can't drive a car. Neither of us can drive."

Removing her hands from the table, Bev leaned back. She crossed her arms. This being nice shtick was turning out to be a lot more of a pain in the ass than she suspected.

Somewhere in the back of her mind she pictured them both in a sack, being tossed into the river, like a bag of giant unwanted puppies.

"How about we take them, drive them somewhere," Sophie wasn't getting up yet. Instead she was holding the hand of the older lady. Sophie was good at this being kind nonsense, but Beverly knew Sophie wasn't as good as Bev was.

"No, Agent Blackwell." Bev said. She tried to look as if she were conferring instead of arguing or leading. "We have many stops to make. I'm not sure we even have room right now in the car."

She glanced at Lem still in the car by the road.

"Already have some suspects."

Plus, she thought, she couldn't very well take their RV while they were with them. And getting rid of them in the usual way wouldn't be with her new style. It was all so much frustration.

"Maybe we could take them to a nearby store for a bit?" Now Sophia stood up, smiling broadly. "At least until somebody comes for them."

"We're not going anywhere," now the man crossed his arms, pushed back from the card table a bit. "Not until our son gets here. He's the one takes us places."

Senile, Bev thought, they have to be senile. But how could senile people be left like this? How they be getting along if they were so out of it? What the hell was here for them? Didn't make sense.

There wasn't even any other RVs around. No car, no friends. What were they doing here?

Off to her left, she looked down to the river. She could barely make out another wooden sign, this one much larger. It read simply "Rides."

"What the hell…" she caught herself, "excuse me, but can I ask why you're here? I mean, why you spend so much time by the river. By yourself?"

"Run the business, of course, ain't nobody else going to do it." The man was frowning at her.

"Business?" Sophie asked.

Beverly looked at the sign as the man continued.

"Givin' rides! Showin' people around! Helping folks cross over."

Cross over? Bev was expecting more of a hood, a scythe. Maybe a tall dude asking for coins. But they probably didn't mean that.

Probably.

The afterlife did not consist of meeting these two, down by the river. Living in their oversized van.

Probably.

Doubt.

"Tours?" She asked.

"Heavens no," the lady explained. "We mostly ferry people." She smoothed wrinkles in the tablecloth. "Not that there's a lot of call for that."

"Why would you ferry people?" Sophie looked down at the two, her face compassionate, "when there's a bridge right down the road? They could just drive over, right?"

"Let's…" Grandma started, then "I know what, Oscar, let's get out that Risk game. You love it so, and we can play while we wait for Henry to arrive."

"Henry?"

"Our son," she replied. "He comes to check on us." She patted her husband's hand. "He'll know what to do. He always does."

The man nodded absently. "Can't just be running off anywheres."

Bev shifted her weight, trying to hide her impatience. "But that could take hours! When's he coming?"

"Oh sometime," she replied, "before dark. Usually."

Bev looked to the car. Mack was not happy.

"Oh dear," Bev looked with worry at Sophie, then back to the seated couple. "Mack, our supervisor, is up there waiting. We may get in a lot of trouble if we can't get you to safety."

They wanted to be kind. Fine, Bev thought. She'd be their puppy. She'd wag her tail if she had to. Just get moving.

The old man had made it to standing, looking back to his seated wife.

Beverly slouched; her options were getting even more limited.

"Risk? Or not Risk?"

"Tsk tsk, that is SUCH a shame," she stood also.

Now we're getting somewhere.

"We don't want to get these two in trouble."

Honk! Honk!

Bev looked to see Mack reaching inside the car, leaning on the horn. He made the hurry-up motion.

Lem was just sitting eyes forward. Odd. Like a statue. He was frowning more than she'd seen him before. Something had rattled him.

"Well, let's move it along then, Susan. They don't have all day!"

But they couldn't fit in the car. And they had no way to leave. Maybe if she took them out in that boat, got them to the deep water, pushed them over the edge? Tied some rocks around them if necessary?

But that wouldn't be nice, would it? Even if the others couldn't see, freaking Mack would *know*. And Beverly would be failing at being nice. Not happening.

Go where?

But they were moving!

"Okay then, Oscar. No need to yell." She started towards the door. "Let me get my purse. You're always yelling about things. Deaf as a doornail…."

Then it happened.

The old lady tripped and fell.

Bev saw her grimace in pain. The man hadn't noticed yet. Ahead, he was halfway up the steps, door open.

"Wow!" Sophia moved immediately over to assist. "Are you okay?"

"Wait," she stopped her, Bev held her hands up in surrender as if to say to Sophie, "Seriously?"

Sophia shrugged. The old guy turned around, dawn breaking on his craggy face.

"Susan? Susan!"

He turned and started down. Bev took the chance to move a little closer to her partner.

"This is not working," she said in a low voice, watching the man come to his wife.

"Be patient, Bev," Sophie replied.

"Not my thing."

She intercepted the man and pulled a zip tie from her back pocket. Grabbed his shoulder. Turned him around.

"Do we need help?" Sophie asked.

"We'll put them in the boat," she replied. "They have a boat, let's use it."

Damn if the old fuck didn't get away from her. Slippery little bugger.

"Dammit! Help me!"

"Leave him alone," Grandma said, getting up. She must be okay, and all three turned their attention to the old man who was struggling with Beverly.

Better and better. Just keeps getting better and better.

Looking at the old guy, she almost didn't hear Sophie.

"Ugh."

At first, Bev couldn't believe what she saw. Turning, the old lady was standing behind Sophie, strangling her with her knitting yarn. Sophie's eyes bulged. Her face was dark red. The lady grinned maniacally.

Without thinking, she picked up the plastic lantern and whacked the old bitch as hard as she could. It wasn't much, but it was enough for Sophie to struggle free. She began rubbing her neck.

The cranky codger, mean old bat didn't go down, though, instead coming at Bev – coming at Bev! – with a knitting needle.

Good thing she still had the lantern.

"Mack!" Sophia said, "Mack! Help us!"

"I got this," she told her partner but didn't dare take her eyes off of grandma. They faced off. It was grandma versus grandma.

Yes! This was the excitement she'd been waiting for!

She could feel, she just knew he was coming over, Mack with that stupid grin on his face.

RV grandma lunged. Beverly blocked with the lantern, but a lantern wasn't much of a weapon against edged attack. She cherished thinking about all her options. If only she could make it slow.

"What do you think, Sophia?" Mack asked from behind.

"Help us," was the reply, "Please."

Mack Azure, unarmed and smiling, reached in to tap RV grandma on the shoulder.

That was it. That was the big attack. Susan Grimes looked at Mack as if she saw a cat juggling. It didn't register with anybody. It was extremely odd.

As he touched her, she collapsed. Bev noticed that there was no cry of pain, no final breath. Mack touched her and that was it.

"You're really not cut out for this, are you?" Sophie asked Bev, and Bev wished Sophie had come at her with the knitting needle instead of RV grandma.

She said nothing.

"Both of you, both," Mack said, emphasizing the word, "did quite well. Beverly here is not as good as she thinks she is, but that is not new. She is progressing quite well."

"We going to let him go?" Sophia asked.

Old dude was busy getting on, beating feet as fast as he could down to the boat.

"He's leaving. That's what you want." Bev said.

Fuck you, Mack.

Sophie laughed just a bit, blowing off tension. She looked at Mack as if expecting more instructions, her rescuer, but he just kept being amused watching the guy leaving.

"Good thing you had me along," Sophie said to her.
Bev would kill them all if she could.
But somehow she'd be nice about it.

19

Victory Parade

THE OLD MEN MEANDERED BY THEM, trying to hold formation and failing, old warriors lost in the old wars existing now only in their memories. They were ahead of the horses and behind the marching band. The team had found a war remembrance parade, and they had great seats. They were stuck in traffic. The first car stopped to let it go by. It might be an hour or more.

"Rejoice!" Mack held out his hands as if leading an invisible choir instead of looking at some horses' asses. "We are all doing quite well and have met all of our goals. The future is bright and happy!"

There were times, rare times when Mack Azure could be serious, contemplative even.

This was not now.

She missed it.

The RV they had commandeered was nice, she had to admit. They'd hooked the cop car to the tow bar and the RV was quite roomy compared to that. It even had a kitchen.

"Do you really think I did well?" She didn't trust his answer worth a damn but she at least deserved to hear it.

"Indeed I do! We are all coming together quite nicely. It won't be long until we're ready for the Ha part of our shuhari. I will embrace it as a good student should."

Lem and Sophie exchanged confused looks. Mack started making a list.

"Both of you," indicating Lem and Sophie, "have begun integrating into our horde, our nest pod. Sophia did a wonderful job with the Grimes although she was almost gutted like a stinking fish left out too long on a sinking boat. Bev is mastering her apprenticeship. Lemuel has stood out the most amongst us all."

"Being gutted like a fish and just hanging out doesn't sound like much progress, Mack," Bev said.

He was undeterred.

"But you are incorrect. You really should stop being so negative, Beverly. I've gotten updates to our travel list and I've been told that management is watching! Management! This is my moment! It is finally happening. Rejoice!"

"Do you think our reset, our talk in the forest, becoming more of a partnership had something to do with it?" She asked him. Please come back old Mack.

"I do. It was an excellent idea on my part allowing you to function as a social guide. We will become famous." He did a lookup. "We will be like your Teenage Mutant Ninja Turtles."

"No, Mack, I don't think we will," she corrected him. Turtles.

He took it in stride, bless him. Another lookup.

"Like Earth, Air, Fire, and Water."

A singing group?

"Maybe not." Mack was a human-shaped bomb. She watched Mack, wondering where the red wire was, not wanting to touch it.

"Then we are the new Chipmunks. We will sing victorious holiday songs alongside Alvin in honor of our accomplishment."

She simply shook her head no. She didn't want to say anything.

She rubbed her numb arm, still useless.

"The Four Horsemen of the Apocalypse?"

She squinched her face. She said nothing.

He smiled, victory won.

"We will need to allow Lem and Sophia to contribute, of course. We are, as they say, on a roll."

He crossed his arms, pleased with himself. He looked like a middle-aged man looking at his just-mowed lawn. To her it was just a yard.

"I have been improving myself. Finally it is working. Tyler is next on our list, Sophia, after the warehouse. We will visit. We will help. You will be happy."

Sophia beamed.

"All of you will love the warehouse," Mack said. "So much activity, coming and going. So many interesting species and cultures. It will be something for you to remember for a lifetime, this one or some other one…"

"You're incorporating us?" Lem asked, "A team? Nest pod? What if we don't want to join up?"

Bev and Lem shared a look, two men in a bar wondering if a fight was going to start, wondering if they were going to be in it.

"Why wouldn't you want to join? What foolishness is that?"

"Mack," Lem said, "things don't always work like you want, do they?"

"Admit it, Mack," Bev said, "all these great things can also be terrible things. You may be misreading our situation."

"I don't want to join anything," Sophia added. "This is terrible. I won't do it. I only want Tyler. You can go jump in a lake."

"You will do as…."

Lem stopped him.

"Mack, do you need to do that right now? Show off?"

"No."

"Then let's make the warehouse, see what happens."

"You are correct. It will not matter much. You will all be dead soon anyway."

"I die now?" Sophie's face was a storm.

"Most assuredly, Sophia and Lemuel, within the next few hours. We will make it pleasant for you."

Mack looked at them as if he'd told a joke they missed.

"We can't continue like this as if two of you are going to be normies, DIMwits. How silly."

Another marching band started clanging and hooting in front of them, out of step, out of beat, but giving it their all anyway.

"I'm going to die," Sophia said. It was not a question.

Lem cocked his head. "Can't you change that?"

"I don't see how. I do not make these rules."

Now Bev crossed her arms. Missed some weeds over there, Mack. Your mower ain't that great.

"Why don't you call management? If everybody's interested in how we're doing why not call them, give it a shot?"

"I tried," Mack let out a breath. "They won't return my calls."

She almost laughed. She stopped soon enough, she hoped.

"So," she said to Mack, "You don't know. You have no idea what it is that you're doing so well at, you don't really know if we're doing the right thing or not, do you? You just know we're gathering interest, somehow, from somebody. Therefore we all die."

"Yes," Mack replied, but he didn't look at them.

"You said we're the cool kids now, we're on a roll." She couldn't help herself. "But here you are, cool kid, admitting Sophie dies, Lem dies, I'm stuck second fiddle, you have no idea what happens. And this is a good thing."

"Yes," he didn't break his smile, "of course it is. I am sure it's difficult for primitives. You simply don't understand it all yet. Small minds and all. I may have to take direct control again, at least until your intelligence improves. I will do what I must."

"Mack," she said, "look around. Whatever's happening here is a social thing. It's not just you. It was your great god-like decision, of course, you being the wondrous legendary all-powerful Mack Azure, but this is the social thing. Remember that? You promised. Social things are my area. You agreed."

"Fine then, instead of this, I will continue in this new way," he said, still looking ahead, still smiling at something. The only thing to see were people walking along with pooper-scoopers picking up the animal crap. He was smiling at his own joke long gone that nobody laughed at.

"Admit it," she said. "Everything is basically the same. When did all of these good things begin?"

"When we caught those two," he sounded almost petulant.

And the smile was gone. And he looked back to them. And that was the only thing he really knew. She got it. The only thing that happened was picking up these two from a filthy dumpster behind a bowling alley. Mack was only an idiot, a very lucky idiot, and everybody knew it, including his bosses.

"I am profoundly sad."

"Get over it," she told him.

When she was a child, Bev remembered seeing somebody very evil appearing in a movie. They were so dark and powerful their entire body was white, like they were their own negative image.

Mack looked this way. He was glowing so hot she could feel the heat from several feet away and was sure the inside of the RV would catch fire any second. Mack glowed white. He burned.

Lem scuttled towards him as if Mack were a fire and Lem was trying to keep his hands warm. He'd burn himself.

"I WILL LAY WASTE TO THIS ENTIRE AREA THE WAY I DID WITH THE BLACK DEATH. I CANNOT CONTINUE LIKE THIS. THIS SPECIES IS IN NEED OF A RESET."

The Black Death? Millions of people dead, a third of Europe gone?

Thousands of dead bodies rotting in the street? Mack had caused the Black Death?

The Winnebago shook.

Lem got within reaching distance of Mack but observed him closely. He was only inches away.

Lem looked at Mack kindly. Damn if Lem didn't look sad.

"Maybe you should relax more, take up some sort of art."

Mack started deflating.

"I have already taken your advice. I have tried. Your planet has always frustrated and puzzled me, even when I kept many of you as pets." He said in a lower voice, still not conversational, "Enough of this."

Now Lem touched him, just lightly on the shoulder. Surprise? Fear? Shock? Mack was electrocuted. He was extinguished. The fire went out.

"Hey Mack, don't sweat it. I've got this."

"I am unsure, unhappy."

Was that Mack? What the hell? Self-fucking-doubt?

"Can you give it a few more days? See where you end up? Chill a bit?"

"I don't know."

Bev could have never pulled that move with Mack. It was crazy. But Lem could.

How.

"Do that, trust me. I've got you covered."

Bev thought it was like watching the sun break out from a cloud, or a total eclipse disappearing in the ether. Dark became light, without warning, only it was the other way.

"Then I will return. We will return to our previous place, small simpletons. As I said, rejoice. We are happy."

Mack switched to smiling again, but it was an empty smile. He was the only one smiling.

They waited for the parade to end. It seemed forever.

Slowly the inside temperature faded back to normal. Bev was relieved that there was no fire. Dying in one week was trouble enough, damned if she wanted to do it twice.

20

Getting Into It

THE GUARD AT THE GUARD SHACK said there was no getting in right now, and that was that. Here's your pager. Don't call us, we'll call you.

That was the way all star clusters worked, Mack assured them as they searched for a place to take a break. They were always busy. It was always hurry up and wait. They watched dozens of trucks enter and leave. Centralized Distribution Center, it was called, or CDC. Didn't look like a star cluster to Bev, whatever that was. Looked like a warehouse. All the different kinds of trucks coming and going, all the different company names – maybe CDC was a better name.

Still, warehouse.

Mack knew a place they could chill, and before too long Sophia was in the Winnebago making sandwiches. Mack had stepped off to make another one of his cell calls. And while he schmoozed and schemed his way through whatever corporate bullshit he was up to lately – she noticed that there on the little card table he had left the keys to the patrol car and the RV.

Keys.

There were people close by. Not a lot, but if she ran to the car and made a scene she'd easily be visible to a couple of dozen. The thing he was afraid of fucking with, a crowd.

Might be enough.

She was getting close. She could feel it. There was a big old cruise ship, full of fun and games – Bev's fun and games – finally pulling into her port. Can't jump on yet. Too soon and she'd drown. But the ship was close. She heard the music. She saw the dancing.

"Hey," Sophie yelled from inside the RV, "I can't carry all of this. Might take me a couple of trips."

"Oh dear," she smiled and winked at Lem. He was beginning to pay attention to his surroundings.

He remained impassively looking at her. She was a show on the Discovery Channel he wasn't interested in but was too lazy to actually change the channel.

She went to the RV door.

"Let me help, sweetie," she went in, grabbed some of the food Sophie had made, and returned back to the table.

Lemuel remained stoic.

"Are you okay, Lem?" she asked. She checked his head for a fever. "You've been pushing yourself a lot. Sophia tells me it's not pleasant if you overdo it. Here, let me get a washcloth."

She went in, dampened a cloth and put it on his head. He returned a bit from his reverie, smiling at her and saying thank you.

She sat.

"You see," she said to him, "I'm not the stereotypical evil person you might imagine. Don't believe everything you read in the paper."

"You keep saying that. I don't think I can imagine…" he began, then changed direction, reassessed. "You've been trying, Beverly. I'll give you credit for that. And you're making good progress."

He looked at her like he'd just taught his pet cow to sing. It went against its nature. Beverly Castler, yodeling bovine.

She swallowed her pride and simply nodded her thanks. She *had* been trying, that much was true. And somehow she felt better knowing that he noticed.

"I've been thinking," Sophie said as they both engaged in conversation, relieved not to be staring each other down. "Mack seems afraid of crowds, and we have these."

Sophie almost glared at Mack. Muscles tightened in her jaw. Her eyes narrowed. She didn't blink. She was clear and determined.

She pointed to the keys. Bev couldn't help but look over to make sure Mack hadn't noticed.

He hadn't.

Sophie continued, "How about me and Bev take the keys, make a run for the car? Maybe we could run over him before he did something."

"No. Absolutely not," she said to almost the exact idea she'd been thinking minutes before. "Mack – can do things. I saw him almost shoot up a crowd of children who only wanted ice cream. Remember the old lady? He still has that gun. I don't think he'd be shy about using it."

"I don't like it," Lem said, instantly disliking the idea. "How about that gun? Why didn't he shoot them up? The ice cream people. What stopped him?"

Mack was imperfect, Bev thought. She didn't say it. He has flaws inside that I've been carefully exploring, she thought, and you haven't. You're not even a good slacker.

"I don't know. He's very strange." was what she gave them. Neither one of them were smart enough to think past that.

Perhaps.

Sophie gave up on arguing with Bev's no; instead she turned to Lem's indecision.

"You said you were in this no matter what," she said. "You said we'd both figure it out."

She moved her head a bit indicating Mack.

"If we don't get rid of him we'll never get anywhere."

Now she looked at Bev.

"Even if he shoots all of us in the process."

Whoa, Bev thought, but before she could say anything Lem responded to Sophie.

"I'm not hurting anybody," he said. "I'm not hurting anybody!"

But Bev could see Lem frown. She could see a storm under his eyes. Bev knew Lem, maybe better than he knew himself.

Must make note of that.

Sophia reassured him gently. "I'll handle whatever needs to be done. She stopped patting. "I'll do my best."

That seemed enough. Lem simply nodded.

Bev's cruise ship was sailing past the port, heading directly towards an iceberg. She watched it go.

She swallowed. She nodded a bit slowly as if considering Sophie's ideas.

She was not considering Sophie's ideas, but she did her best to look like she was.

"So, we grab the keys," Lem offered Sophie, "somehow we get away. What then?"

Sophia looked at Beverly, uncomfortable to say much, going with "we grab Tyler, you know, and the things," another sharp glance to Bev then back to Lem. "That should give us, er, the things we need."

"Hmmm," Bev said. She took her reading glasses off, cleaned them a bit, then carefully put them in the exact spot on her nose as they watched. "You could make a break for it. That might work. You guys might be on to something."

Bev looked at the table. She was simply a humble person considering the ideas of these two wise children.

Let them try, she thought. She'd watch. More for her to learn.

"She's lying," Lem concluded, "she couldn't care less about us. She'd be happy watching us fail."

"Not true," Bev lied. "I'm doing my best to be a good person."

"You are doing your best," he agreed. "Keep working on it." Looking to Sophie, "I can make a distraction."

Unable to resist her curiosity, Beverly looked at Mack, still on the phone. Does he know?

Seeing them look, he smiled.

Sophie pointed to the food she'd brought out as if asking, "Interested? Coming for food?"

Mack nodded, still chatting, and made the "couple minutes" gesture. He then returned to his call.

There was a loud buzzing, as if the world had begun vibrating.

What the hell was that?

Again.

Searching, she found the buzzer. They were paged. It was their turn. Time to head back.

Now back to Mack. He hadn't heard it yet.

With one move, Lem swiped the pager, off the table, under the RV.

"Found this inside," Sophie held up a second wire-bound spiral notebook, the kind schoolchildren used, like she already carried.

"What is it?" Bev asked.

"Our answer."

"You in or not," Lem looked at Bev. His eyes told her that the time of fakery was over.

She squirmed. As much of a pain as Mack was, somehow Lem was worse, and he wasn't even a crazy demonic mastermind. He was just some dumbass broken Boy Scout. Mack could do most anything, and this runt could do most nothing.

And yet he was the one. Somebody needed to look out after him. He was the real teacher.

Beverly's ship had hit the iceberg. Sink or swim, Beverly.

She didn't want to answer, so she didn't. She froze her face, deep in a poker game with herself. The game was going badly.

Sophia looked at Lem. She was still holding the notebook.

"Something bad happens," Sophie said, "Tyler."

Lem looked far away. He nodded.

"Well then," grabbing the car keys first, Sophie stood. She purposefully walked over to Mack, notebook in hand.

He hung up, held his arms apart. Friend.

"On hold," he said, explaining the wait.

"I have some calligraphy here you might be interested in," she said, holding the notebook out, "also some exercises you might want."

"Why I certainly do, Sophia! Thank you!"

She began to hand him the notebook, then it fell on the ground. "Oops."

As he bent to get it, Sophia deftly pivoted around, pulled Mack's gun from the holster, and backed away pointing it at him.

Sophie had the gun.

"Sophia Blackwell!"

Mack's face was red. His fists were balled.

There was electricity in the air.

"BEVERLY CASTLER! ASSIST ME!"

Bev's mouth hung open. She looked around, seeing them all for the first time.

Sophie was still backing up, pointing the gun at Mack.

Go weak, she thought.

"Me? I'm just an old lady. I couldn't help anybody."

It was if she'd told them all a joke. They all smiled in spite of the tension.

What the fuck was funny?

"I'll settle this." Lem had a butter knife and was trying to get around her.

She grabbed the knife from him.

"You'd never make it," she said, not even bothering to address him, her eyes fixed on the battle between Mack and Sophie.

Well there's a fine pickle you've gotten yourself into, Bev thought.

But instead of shooting, Sophie took the gun and threw it.

By this time both Bev and Lem were moving towards them, halfway there.

Bev was a step ahead, and Lem couldn't catch a cold, so she caught the gun.

Now Bev had the gun, what she wanted all along. Mack and Sophia both glared at her: you going to fix this, or are you going to fix this?

A clanking to her right. Sophie eyebrows went up. Trouble.

She glanced quickly. Lem was splayed out on the ground, seizing.

Bev wasn't about to give that new crisis more than a second's attention. Mack was slowly walking towards her, still with that smile, as if he knew exactly what she'd do.

Somebody had to look out after him.

She pushed the gun torward Mack.

"You," she said with dead eyes. "In the trunk. I'll shoot you where you stand. Now."

He leaned forward just a bit more, as if testing her, then realized the gig was up. Come at her and she'd kill him.

Rattling continued to her side, jerking around, Lemuel deep in his defect, one of many.

Mack nodded quickly, as if agreeing, turned and went back to the trunk. Sophia came over and opened it for him.

That was her mistake. Sophia's last one.

Getting in, Mack breezed by Sophia. He touched her in only the slightest way.

She dropped.

There was no more Sophia Blackwell.

"You're always with the surprises, aren't you Mack?" She came a bit closer, still far out of his reach. "Now shut yourself in the trunk."

He did as requested.

She looked at the gun. She looked at the lump of Sophia. The metallic rattle behind her was getting weaker.

Lem needed her. Sophie didn't need anybody. She never would.

Putting the gun in her pocket, she went back, got the wet towel, and attended to Lem.

Kneeling beside him, keeping a wary eye on the trunk, she tended to him gently, saying nice things in a soothing voice and making sure his return was peaceful.

He came awake, then almost instantly went to sleep. It was the way, she knew.

Moving back a few feet, still watching the car, she sat at the table, munching on carrot sticks, and considered her options.

Sophie was beside the car. She probably couldn't be seen by the others waiting, but Bev didn't have long. Far under the RV the buzzer buzzed again, reminding her of the time. Lem snored peacefully.

There was a gentle breeze. It was arboreal tranquility, peaceful, sweet, the kind she had as a child.

Seeing him begin to stir, she went back. Within a few minutes he roused, came somewhat awake, and was sitting up, facing her, facing away from the car.

"What happened?"

"I've got the gun," she patted her pocket.

"Mack?"

"Don't have to worry about him," she glanced over his shoulder at the car. Still there.

Seeing her look of concern, he began to turn back to the car. She stopped him.

"Sophie?"

She shook her head no.

"I'm sorry, Lem," and she meant it.

He gritted his teeth, began flexing his muscles, began trying to collect himself to stand.

"You okay doing that? Standing?"

Still angry/serious, he stopped and looked.

"We have work to do."

"I don't see us doing very much, Lem. Maybe run away."

He thought. She continued.

"Joint suicide perhaps?" Ahe asked.

"There's a way, but only for both of us."

"You know these folks have abilities."

"I do."

"And we can't even see what the hell we're dealing with."

"I can. And I can show you how too."

She thought about the gun.

"Where would we go? Where could we hide?"

"We go get Tyler," he replied. "There's gear there that can help us. Tyler can help us."

Unsure of himself, he wobbled.

"Does Tyler know something about this?" she asked, "Does he have special abilities too?"

He nodded.

"We collect Tyler and the gear," he said, summing it up. "We need to find some people. There are folks who will help us. I know that."

He looked at her with a question.

"And you know these people," she asked.

He nodded.

She looked around. They did have the police car. The car would garner some support, some deference, or at least some respect.

Her entire existence in the afterlife has been characterized by her being, she had to be honest, a total dumbass. Mack was right. She didn't know what she didn't know.

Her ship had indeed come in, and her ship's name was Lemuel Rickenbacker.

"Melons."

"Melons?"

"We're about to commit suicide over melons."

He looked at her quizzically.

"And I'm okay with that."

They got back in the car, this time Bev driving and Lem riding shotgun.

Lem had gone around the front, still with the gritted teeth and determination, ignoring Sophia. Bev knew that Lem knew where she was, but Lem was moving on, no time for grief.

There's something there, she thought, not for the first time.

Before they started, "Ha," she said aloud. She wasn't laughing.

"Ha?"

"Ha. There's your Ha for your Shu, Mack."

They heard banging in the back.

"What's that?"

"Mack. He's in the trunk."

"Good."

Also unexpected.

As she started and put it into drive, Mack banged again.

Lem looked back. He yelled.

"Screw you, Mack, and screw whatever you've gotten us into."

They left the Winnebago. They left Sophie. They left their life.

Game on.

Synthesis: Clean Up

THE ROBOT CAME AT THEM, inch-by-inch, arms whirling, crawling along the track. They double-checked the windows then sat quietly, waiting for it.

Beverly could only be still and quiet for so long, though, and nervous energy overtook her as the automated car wash crawled within inches of their car. She began searching around.

She didn't feel like herself.

Lem looked her with a bit of amused befuddlement.

"I saw it when we were in the back," he reached around behind her seat and pulled out a clear bottle, completely full of a light blue fluid. "That okay?"

"Yes. I'll need to wear it on my belt somehow."

She felt around for a place to hook it and then quickly went to the next item.

"How about you?" she said, looking at him as if seeing him for the first time. "We're going to have to do something about you."

Her face slowly dropped into true concern.

"I'm fine," Lem replied.

He seemed unperturbed, happy. Maybe he was taking drugs, Bev thought. Yes, that would do it.

She pulled out the pistol.

"Now if I just had…"

"More bullets for the gun?" he said, holding out spares.

She smiled, not knowing what to say.

"They were in the dashboard," he said.

"Ok, smart boy, how about getting that shotgun loose, finding some shells for us?"

"Working on it."

He didn't look to be working on anything. He didn't even look like he was concentrating on anything.

"Thank you, Lemuel," she said. "You're actually quite helpful, and at the weirdest times."

"I *am* helpful. You should let me help you more."

"Have at it, then. We have a lot to do. Get snapping."

The first sprays of the wash started grinding on the hood of the cruiser.

Bev started counting on her fingers what remained.

"Top of the list. After this we'll do a complete vacuum and detailing – excluding the trunk, of course."

In reply there was bang from the back. Mack was still with them.

"Then we'll need to wipe it down for prints. We need to inventory anything dangerous and take it with us. Maybe other things too. Got to get a new car. We can dump this in the nearest secluded lake."

Lem gestured to the back.

"With Mack still in it?"

"Sure, he'll make it sink better."

Bang again, not as loud.

"I'll find your shells. We can get the shotgun free," Lem said, looking as if he were giving her a special toy that meant nothing to anybody else, "but we're not going to hurt people, right? I won't hurt anybody."

"We're not letting," she stopped. "What do you want us to do, hand out pamphlets at the mall? Of course we're going to hurt people, most likely very many people. We'll have to hurt people before they hurt us."

"No, we won't," he was still happy but she saw the corners of his mouth turn down a bit.

"How about you? You sure? I saw you going at Mack. Were you really going to try to hurt Mack with that butter knife of yours?"

"No, but he didn't know that."

The idea of Lem somehow being a threat to Mack was so self-contradictory it hurt. It felt like jumping into what you thought was a nice pond only to find it ice-cold and murky. You were unprepared. She had to get out, and right away.

There was a little nit, a burr in her mind. A defect.

The carwash brushes hit the car with vigor.

"Why didn't you shoot Sophie and me?" Lem asked, "I understand that you've picked up some new hobby of trying to show that you're good but once you had the gun you could have done anything you wanted."

"Not a hobby. Always good at doing good things, but I was never good at being good. Always wanted to be the one making decisions. Always the one sorting things out into the good and the bad, the working and the defective. I mastered that. It was time to move on."

"So, somebody helped you? You started believing in something greater?"

"Somebody helping me? That's hilarious. No."

She let that hang, then realized it wasn't enough for him.

"Ever hear the term 'theodicy'? It's the question of if there's a god, why does he allow evil in the world? How can an all-powerful good creator allow kids to get cancer? That kind of thing. Always seemed like a stupid question for halfwits to me, but I've come to realize it works in reverse. If the world and universe is random, chaotic, and full of evil or unpleasant things, why is there good? Why do people like you exist, not fervent devout people hoping to look good to some sky god, just folks who have faith and are acting on that faith to make the world a better place? If you want to figure out what one guy in the sky is doing, that's difficult enough, but maybe you can come up with something. But all the people, everywhere, all over the place? There's like millions of you. Believe all kinds of silly-ass things. You're like rats. I keep stepping on you. It's not simply some shared delusion; it's millions of people, over eons of time, striving for some abstract version of good that's all basically the same. Why? At some point, no matter where you are or what you're doing, you realize that it's time to change. There was something there. I saw that. It was my time to change. I need an answer. I want an answer."

"How did you know that? It was time to change, that is."

"I didn't. Life just kept kicking me in the ass until I accepted it."

He was quiet for a long time.

"Life may have a lot more asskicking in store for you, Beverly Castler."

"Great. Like I said, we need to start finding weapons. My ass doesn't like being kicked."

He didn't move a bit.

"You're really good at this sort of thing, aren't you?" he asked.

"Covering my tracks? Why wouldn't I be?" but he wanted more. Lem always wanted more. "I became an expert in not getting caught. Might call it my area of specialty."

"Has it ever failed you? It must have. You did eventually get caught, right?"

"I did. Made the mistake of trusting another serial killer. He'd just gotten out of prison by exploiting some legal technicality or another. It was an error the cops made. Nice legal work. Represented himself. I wanted to help an ex-con that just got out of prison, that's all. Turned out he was an informant."

She almost spat before continuing.

"Serves me right. I'll never make that mistake again."

"But you admit it," Lem said. "You're smart enough to see error. You understand that you make mistakes. You're not perfect."

"My only mistake was being soft, too kind-hearted. I've always had a very strong humanitarian instinct. All I want to do is help people. It's not easy. I struggle."

"We should call the authorities."

Bev made sure she heard him right.

"Paying attention lately? There are no authorities. Who you gonna call, Ghostbusters?"

"There's always authorities."

Smug little bastard.

"Lem," she said, "do you have any idea what might show up if we could do that? You really want to meet some creature more powerful than Mack? It'd be something out of H.P. Lovecraft. My god Lem. No. Just no. We've got enough trouble as it is. Let's not go looking for more."

The wash had finished. They both stared, waiting for the light to change. Both wanted a quick comeback. They wanted to put the other one in their place.

All they had was the light.

And the wait.

Finally Lem spoke.

"How do you make decisions? I mean, when you're in your lair."

"My lair? What do you think, I'm a spider? I don't have a lair, or a den, a bunker, or a secret cave. I have apartments, a townhouse. a few homes. a timeshare in Florida. I don't have henchman, or minions. I don't twirl a moustache."

She looked at him.

"How did you think I made decisions?"

"From the news and what people said," Lem said, "I was thinking a crystal ball or something like the Eye of Sauron. Maybe you had a magic mirror."

"Sounds like you. You got to give up this superstitious melodrama and be welcomed into adulthood with the rest of us. How about you? How do you make decisions?"

He considered.

"I relax. I listen. I use my spirit. I have faith and trust."

"Doesn't seem to be working too well for you, does it?"

"Perhaps," he said, "How well is your system working for you?"

Her grip tightened on the wheel. She wanted to tear it out of the dash, rip it into the street. Beat him with it. Frozen from the torso up, she cut her eyes sharply. She dared not move her head.

"Something's wrong with me, Lem," she said through gritted teeth. "Something's broken."

Now she faced him.

"And you're the one that broke it."

Lem managed to look kinder than he already was.

"Just relax. It's growing pains. It'll pass."

The light changed. Beverly Castler couldn't put the car into gear. She stared at the dashboard. She tested her one-handed grip. Everything was fine. She just couldn't. Something was missing. A piece had fallen out of her.

"Beverly," he said, "Be honest. Admit it. You didn't just become overwhelmed by life, you made a decision. Your explanation was smoke. You decided to be good."

"I decided because life overwhelmed me. That okay with you? Don't be a moron. You interest me. You and your magic spirit animal nonsense. Here we are. What does The Force tell you now? Who has the list of things to do? Who knows all of this stuff? Who can cover our tracks? Who's the master strategic chess player in this partnership?"

"You are. You got me, you're the master," he said. "But look around you. This ain't chess. You're moving chairs around on the Titanic, that's all."

"Okay. Point taken. Maybe. But there are big decisions and there are little decisions. Big things we can decide later. Right now we need to fix this and make it right."

"Bev, I don't understand you. What's there to fix?"

"This. The lot of this. The car. What are you, crazy?"

"Aren't you the one that told me about the layers of reality?" he said.

She nodded. She wanted to scream at him.

"So," Lem pointed around the car and the exterior with one of his two good hands. "Again, what's there to fix?"

In that moment Bev found that if she tried really, really hard, she could get her left arm to move. It was coming back.

She found that out because she was going to strangle that shaky little metal runt, and she was going to enjoy it.

It was futile. She gave up.

"I need this. Let me do this to save our lives."

"You need to…" he shook his head unable to finish.

Shut the hell up, Lem, she thought.

"I need to…" she repeated, "I need to do this."

She looked around. She was desperate for an escape route.

There were none. All she had was stand and fight.

"I need this…to be sane."

Thank God he didn't go at her again. She couldn't have taken it.

Instead he started down a new path.

"Do you want us to have a partnership you trust, work together?"

"Absolutely," she replied, relieved. "That's the only chance we've got, and it's not much of one."

"Then why are you so bad at it?"

"Bev? Still there? Why can't you work with other people? Work well with them, like a boyfriend-girlfriend but without all the romance? Close? Family?"

The shotgun was nice, she thought idly. It was a favorite of hers, a 12-gauge pump-action. It was a Greener. 12-inch barrel…

Stopped.

He deserved an answer.

"I've always had, I don't know what people call it, trust issues? That's how I got caught."

"But trust is a requirement of a loving partnership. You have to relax, give yourself up to it."

She had nothing but her words. They came from her heart.

"I've never done that before, not really," she said timidly. "It doesn't make sense. It won't fit in my head."

A chill. Back in the frozen pond. Yuck. Murky. Ice. Get out. Now.

"I know," Lem said. "It doesn't. But it's still true."

"Lem, I don't think I can do that, not really. How about I fake it?"

"And now, finally, we're getting into the real work here. This is what we need to do to help." He pointed to her. "You. You're the work."

"If you say so," she managed, "doesn't seem like it from where I'm sitting."

"Bev, I fix the things that are broken. I find the things that can't be found. I help the people that can't be helped. That's my specialty."

"Lem, I'm trying. Don't push me. This all sounds like so much crazy nonsense, ever since I died. What do you want to do next, then, bring Mack into our circle of trust?"

"You like working with Mack?"

"Getting a bit tired of him putting me and everybody else down."

"Yeah," Lem replied, "but he means well. He's very happy and like-able. I think he can help us."

"Oh. My. God. Seriously?"

"Mack's our way forward," he said. "We're going to need to accept him, trust him, forgive him, even love him if we're serious about what we're doing."

"The fuck we do. Damn, kid, that's crazy, even for you."

"Bev, I need Tyler's location," he said. He shrugged and got sad for a minute, then recovered. "I forgot it. Can you at least deal with that, give it a start? Just start the journey. You and I will get there, together. I promise."

"Mack? Lem, you haven't seen such a pain in the ass in your life until you've worked with Mack. He's insufferable, dangerous, insane, untrustworthy…"

Lem stopped her by holding up his hand.

"Yes or no?"

She let out a very long sigh, rolled her eyes, then shrugged.

Finally she nodded.

He waited. He wanted her to say it.

"Yes. Yes, Lem, I will try this emotional commitment nonsense, even though, as I said, I can't do it. And it's crazy."

She wanted to say, "And you're crazy," but didn't.

She let go of the wheel, doubled checked her bottle.

He smiled at her and patted her like she was a baby learning to walk. She wasn't mad. God help her, she liked it. She liked being patted?

"That's good, Bev," he said, "You don't have to."

"If you say so, I'll believe you: He's all we've got."

22

The Melons Speak

TURNED OUT THERE WERE MELONS, TWO FOR A DOLLAR.
It was a different Mack Azure that Beverly saw when they opened the trunk at the fruit stand, and it was a different Beverly Castler looking at him.

She immediately backed up. She wasn't about to let him do to her what he did to Sophie.

"I've got him," Lem said, reaching in.

"Sure?"

"He's not going to hurt me," Lem replied.

And he didn't.

Bev drove them to the nearest big city box store. They weren't going to go flaunting themselves around in public, but she figured that the beat-up parking lot close to all of this other activity was a nice place that would be both public and private. The parking lot was part of an old, dilapidated restaurant stuck on the end of a half-assembled strip mall across the street from the local state police barracks, fast food all over the place. In the parking lot fruit vendors had set up stands. Two melons for a dollar. Nice cover.

Melons were gone, though. Vendors were gone. Long gone. Wrong time of year. They backed into a slot. It was hidden from the barracks.

"Let's get you out of here." Lem managed to help Mack even though Mack was the one who should have been helping Lem. "You okay? Can I get you some water?"

Beverly wasn't getting anywhere near that.

"I'm quite fine. Thank you." Mack was not smiling. He was not boisterous. He looked very serious and appreciative. He looked like he was admiring Lemuel.

Maybe Lemuel wasn't really Lemuel, maybe he was something else, she thought, and a wave of doubt washed over her. She let it pass.

They got him into the abandoned stand, door still open. There they could talk, be very close to help, yet not be bothered. It was the best she could come up with. She'd made sure the door stayed open and she stayed near it.

"I suppose there will be traffic coming and going, police," she said.

Mack looked away, doing one of his data lookups.

"There are three cars within a mile. Observe."

When Beverly was a child, she'd seen the first Star Wars movie, the one with the Princess Leia hologram. She remembered thinking how cool it would be to project fully-formed images in 3D in front of them.

And now she saw one herself.

A little model of the three of them appeared in the shack. It zoomed out, the shack got smaller, the barracks came into view. Finally it zoomed out again, showing a mile circle, roads and imagery. Three cars were labeled. It was the Star Wars version of Google Maps. Mack rotated the image around. Once he made sure they saw the cars, it went away.

"Very cool," Lem said. "You're consistently amazing me, Mack. But you don't like Mack, do you? You'd prefer your real name, your royal name."

"Mack is all we have for this location, this body configuration," Mack said. "My real name is unpronounceable, so 'Mack' will do. I can create more of these images if you desire. I have an almost limitless ability to provide data on the activities on this planet."

Bev thought that Mack sounded like he was giving a middle school book report.

"How much of it can we trust?" she said, but it was if she wasn't there. Mack was focused entirely on Lem even though Beverly was the one holding the gun. She'd try but this was really tough. Lem asked a lot.

"You may require," he began, then restarted. "To provide you with the orientation you need, you are going to become very uncomfortable, angry, unhappy, disillusioned, and despondent with the framing."

Now he sounded like a soldier reporting back from a battle, we're losing the war. He didn't sound like the Mack Azure she'd met just days ago.

Mack glanced at her, took in her doubts, and continued talking to Lem.

"I am happy to serve as a local guide. You'll find that I can help you in ways you will find useful."

"Lem," she almost reached him to grab him before he seriously started considering Mack's words, "This is an awful idea."

Lem kept his eyes on Mack, not in suspicion or fear, but in concern. He spoke to Beverly.

"He's the only one that knows about Tyler, where the school is, what to do next. He'll do what he can to help."

"Yeah, but I still get a very bad feeling about it."

"You're going to want to know about Tyler, Sophia. You're going to want to know why things are the way they are." Now Mack was finally addressing both of them, "But I must provide you background. You must be oriented. You'll need that for the rest, the end."

Lem looked back to Bev. Bev nodded.

"Okay," Lem told him.

The 3D scene returned. This time it was a scraggly old man, unwashed, wearing homespun garments, beard unkempt, finding his way around an old city, manure on the ground. It was clear he was both drunk and confused.

"You probably know this man as Socrates. Syphilic, insane, delusions of grandeur. But he was popular in his day with the youth and he could turn a phrase."

Bev crossed her arms.

"What's Socrates got to do with anything? He was really smart. Got it."

Mack looked sad. It was like watching a fish flounder on the dock. Mack struggled.

"Helps to have friends write your story after you die, that's what."

Lem asked Mack. "So where we are, the problems we have, this all has something to do with Socrates?"

Mack looked to Lem, caught in his lie.

"No. They have to do with the fact that nothing of what you know or believe is real, at least not in the way you understand it. You're all living in a fantasy world of your own creation. This will prevent your acceptance of what comes next."

"Really. I understand quite a bit, jerk," she couldn't help herself no matter how contrite Mack was being.

"History's inaccurate? That's not news. Everybody knows that as we learn more, we know more about history. Maybe you can give us a presentation later."

"You don't know the half of it," Mack replied.

"Lem," she said, "he lies. Don't trust him."

Bev felt like a horrible thing, a fearsome dark shape deep in the abyss, deep in that pond she was stuck in, was about to overcome them, and she had no idea what it was. She knew it would eat her. Sometimes they get in the works.

Fish don't flounder voluntarily. Something yanks them out of the water.

Lemuel Rickenbacker examined Mack Azure much in the same way an entomologist would appraise a new bug.

"He's not going to lie to me, are you?"

Mack shook his head no, but slowly, as if testing. What was he testing?

Lem backed up a bit, studying more, and almost lost his balance and fell over.

Bev caught him immediately.

He was smiling. He looked at her, gently patted her hand.

"Thank you," as if he were the one being kind to Beverly.

Bev went back to looking at Mack, now closely.

"If he's going to help, even if it involves some history lesson, first I want him to show us where Tyler is. That's a simple question with a simple answer." Bev felt very nervous. She was not used to that feeling. It almost felt like...worry.

A brick sign appeared in their 3D space, the kind they might put in front of the local doctor or dentist's office.

"École pour les petits fous," the sign out front read.

French, she thought, that would be either Louisiana or Quebec. They wouldn't have taken Tyler overseas.

She could look it up.

"Now show me Tyler," Lem said.

Mack made the looking-up motion, then gritting his teeth.

"I can't."

This was unexpected. Beverly came closer not thinking of the danger he represented.

"Why?" She asked.

"I don't know," he finally admitted as he stopped trying. "I'm being blocked by a higher power."

"A higher power?" Bev was angry and didn't know why. "All this Guardian shit, the rules, the tradition, the bar, all this work you've had me doing, all of that – and now you're playing the higher power card? Now? This is all just another level of the same shit we already got here?"

He nodded.

Now it was Beverly's turn to let her anger overtake her.

Lem smiled, she caught him, but only a bit, as if he'd heard an off-color joke in another room and was doing his best not to respond to it.

"So you think you're our only hope?"

Mack straightened up, squared his shoulders, back to familiar territory. Bev saw the old Mack peeking through.

"There is no chance of survival without my help. I will help you small, insig…little people survive your journey."

"He's lying. He killed Sophia!" She knew both of these people, deep in her heart, Lem and Mack, and they were confusing the hell out of her.

Lem peered.

"No, he's not."

"Did you hear him start to insult us just now? Have you heard him all along? How much can you take, Lem? You want him to summon up Jesus, or your parents, start showing you how broken they were? How messed up everything we think is?"

Two people appeared. They were in a kitchen preparing a meal. The phone rings. The lady goes to answer it.

"I know my parents," Lem said. "You can show me nothing there."

The scene disappeared in smoke and was replaced by an emaciated man, sitting against a stone wall.

"This is Jesus, son of Joseph," Mack said, "Although you know him by many other names…"

"Gimme the gun," Lem held his hand out.

"Sure," she gave it without thinking. It was probably safer with Lem than her. It was a very strange thought on a very strange day.

Mack froze the scene.

"Mack," she asked, "can't you find anything good? Anything hopeful?"

"You are defective and primitive," he said immediately without thinking. He didn't continue.

Bev looked at Lem, then Mack.

Mack spoke.

"I have nothing for you but the truth."

Lem shot Mack, and Mack died. There was no drama, no emotion. There was a sharp bang and it was done. It could have been a car backfiring.

"You know," Lem said, putting the gun away and looking back to her, "you were right. Mack was a real downer."

"Well just ain't that a mess," a new voice said with a deep rural accent.

They both turned to see the new man behind them at the door.

The first thing Bev noticed was that he wore a straw hat. Perhaps he owned the fruit stand.

Then she took in the bib overalls: new, clean, and neatly pressed. There was a monogrammed name on the front pocket. A pipe stuck out. There was a watch with a chain.

"I'm James Robert Smith," he said, patting his chest as if he had suddenly just discovered that he had a body.

It was a corncob pipe. In gold thread the monogram read, "Jim-Bob."

"I'm the Jim-Bob what that runs the Jim-Bob's House of Corncobs," he seemed quite proud of himself. "But you may know me better as Nexel Five-Bone."

He stepped in.

"I've been waiting a long time for this."

23

Nexel Five-Bone

Looking back later, Beverly remembered Jim-Bob as a perfect cross between a dumb redneck southern farmer and James Bond. He was all cornpone shucks and gee-whiz, but every now and then there was a glimpse of steely ball-bearing missile eyes, many more than just two, an alien superintelligence dark, deep, faraway, and playing with a meat puppet named Jim-Bob with one finger from a vast distance the way a small child might poke at an anthill with a stick while role-playing Godzilla and thinking about dinner. Not very interesting.

"Cleaned up at the RV for ya, now followed y'all here," he said cocking his straw-hat big head, putting his thumbs in his bibs, and stepping in a bit to look around. He looked like he was buying a cow. Or melons.

"You-all been busy!"

He turned to face Lem.

"Pretty much things on schedule. We-all ready to deploy the first units. Give the word. We've even got a temporary command center, such that it is."

Beverly and Lem shared a confused look.

Seeing their confusion, the man/thing stepped back a bit, tilted his head back, and smiled, the way one might do in order to only show their upper teeth.

"Aw," he said, resuming his former stance and then placing his arms akimbo. "I guess y'all got some questions. I may have come too soon. Dadburn it!"

"Ya think," Bev replied.

He answered Lemuel.

"Been following you since you came to my House of Corncobs," he said.

Bev couldn't help herself.

"You run a House of Corncobs?"

Nods.

"But of course you do. Why …"

"I don't want to bother you," Lem interjected, "and please tell me if it's too much trouble.."

Everybody looked at him.

"Could I please have a corncob pipe?"

"Why a-course you can," Jim-Bob/Nexel replied, handing him the one from his overalls. "This here's one of my best models: TR-1700."

Lem held it out as he received it, admiring it. Nexel saw him.

"Nice, isn't it?" Lem said to both of them.

Neither could adequately reply, each for their own reasons. The room was silent.

Finally, and with difficulty, Lem put his new pipe away. He looked at Mack.

"We're going to need to do something about the body," he began shifting and shuffling towards it, "It's my responsibility."

"Nope nope nope," Nexel briefly gave up the act and came quickly the rest of the way into the room. "I've got it."

He drug Mack's heavy body to the door. It was a strain. He took out his handkerchief wiped his brow.

"Whee-dog, he heavy! I'll put him in the wagon in a minute. Anything else need to be done right away?"

Beverly clasped her chest. If this was going to be ham theater night she was going to have a nice big slice of it.

"Thank goodness we have somebody here to sort things out," she said, gushing.

Nexel looked at her. It was the first time.

"I don't understand," he said.

Lem patted her on the shoulder, the way one might pat a beloved friend at the funeral home.

"I don't think she would either," he said, and before she could reply he pointed to Mack's body and said, "I'm going to need to see his manager."

Nexel looked at Lem.

"Not here," Nexel replied.

Lem nodded slowly.

"My goodness," Bev said, "Stars alive, what in heaven's name are both of you going on about? We certainly have us a Karen here, don't we?"

She almost said, "It's bound to give me the vapors," but she didn't want to overplay it. She was unsure of how this puppet affectation game worked.

They were playing at something, she now knew, but she didn't know all the rules. What she did know was that whatever this game was, she was born for it. She knew it. An entire lifetime, she was finally in her element.

"Everybody got a boss, little lady," she thought he sounded so pedantic that he might next offer to buy a piece of bubblegum for her.

She looked to Lem.

"You mean the guy on the cellphone? You can meet him?"

"Well there, ya can," Nexel replied, "if you want to, and it sure looks like you're a fixin' to, but that ain't easy."

Nexel let out a long, long breath. It was a time before he inhaled again.

"I don't recommend it," he said.

Bev ignored him, instead continuing with Lem.

"Mack's got a phone," she gestured to the body. "If you're determined to blow things up, why don't we simply pick it up and call the guy? Last number dialed. See who answers."

She felt a chill, a breeze.

She started towards the door where Mack lay, but Nexel stopped her, quite forcefully.

"Outta all the bad ideas, little lady, this is the worst. Trust me. Aw shucks." He looked to Lem, "we're not prepared," he said in a completely different tone.

She backed up and crossed her arms, taking it all in, considering her next move.

She felt something poke at her side.

Lem was holding the gun. Poking her to get her attention, he gave it back.

He had a sheepish smile.

She could hear the wind picking up, then looking to the door saw it begin to whip dust around. Could be a storm coming.

"Getting risky here. We're going to need to move along," she said to both of them, "or at least take it to a better spot."

"Agreed," James Bond Jim-Bob Hillbilly Nexel replied, but again to Lem and not her. "What are your instructions?"

"Why would I have instructions?" Lem asked.

The wind kept coming, more and more, the storm unlikely to hold off much longer.

Finally Lem said, "Oh."

Bev looked at Nexel, Jim-Bob, James Bond, Corn fuck, whoever the hell he was.

"You mean you're not here to rescue us?"

"Rescue you?" he asked. "You-all the ones going to rescue us!"

She uncrossed her arms, put one hand on her hip. She looked at him the way somebody might look at the pizza boy who yet again brought their pizza an hour late.

"Do we look like we can rescue anybody?"

Nexel looked around the shack, seeing the unseen.

"Yes."

"You're starting to sound like Mack," she told him. "I don't like that."

"Let's just say that we're all going to need to work on our communications skills," Lem said as if he were addressing his new employees. "Synergy can only happen when we speak truth to power."

Nexel nodded as if this were great advice.

Bev was having none of it. She laughed but stopped.

"What's next? Are we going to have an encounter session? You two need a room?"

Lem caught himself, not laughing but struggling with not-laughing. It was the wrong time and the wrong place. She didn't understand it. But she liked it.

Bev gestured at both Mack and Nexel.

"I thought you were all together, on the same team."

Nexel smiled.

"Nyah, we're the other guys. Shoulda come in on a horse. Got a white one and everything. Can't get him to stay in the shop, though. He was always complaining 'bout something or 'nother. Dang horses."

"I don't wanna do this." Lem looked at the ground and nobody else.

It was her turn to comfort Lem. She placed her hand on him.

"I know, right? But nobody seems to ask us."

She watched him look back and forth, searching the empty ground. He finally looked up to Nexel.

"We're going to need that Scrambler," Lem said.

"What's a Scrambler?" Bev felt like she was talking to Mack again, that first day. Every question's answer only led to new questions.

"Remember when you told me about the layers, the transparencies?" Lem asked.

"Sure. Reality is a big overhead projector and what we see on the wall depends on the transparency layers we put on it."

"A Scrambler is a device that lets you choose," he said. "This USI thing you were talking about, Scramblers put you in charge of the projector, not the USI."

"That's right," Nexel said. "Been working on this for a looooooong time. We've began production, field testing. I believe you've seen it in action."

Lem nodded but Bev was the one replying.

"Why would anybody want to do that? Why would anybody want one of those? One reality is hella complicated enough."

"Beverly," Lem said, "I'm beginning to love you, truly I am. And Nexel Five-Bone would tell us how important it is and why; I'm certain of that. He's an open book, at least to me. But I don't think you'd understand. I'm just beginning to."

Lem straightened up, at least as best as he could. He looked at Nexel with as much seriousness as Bev had ever seen.

"I'm going on alone," he said.

"The hell you are," Beverly said.

"Sure? You're coming with me?" Lem said, unsure he'd heard correctly, "Just us two?"

"I'm coming with."

"Why?"

"To be honest, Lemuel, I have no idea. I know I'm supposed to do this, to go on with you, more than anything else I've ever known."

"Nexel," Lem said. "Why the corncob shop? Why make a store like that?"

"These conceits work great," he said. "If you know the USI, you know you're among friends, or at least fellow sentients. It's an inside joke. If you don't get it, you simply think it's another one of those oddball and strange shops that pop up, last a year or two, and then go broke. Worst-case, you come in and buy something made of corncobs. Once you're inside, we figure out who you are."

"Makes sense."

Gone was the hillbilly from before.

"Can't I come along?"

"No," Lem said. "Where I'm going you can't follow."

"How about he keeps trailing on along behind us, Lem?" Bev was unsure of her future no matter what happened but she'd like Lem to at least cover their options, have a fallback plan.

"No," he said simply and then to Nexel, "go back to your work, Nexel. I'll contact you when I'm ready, when things are…prepared."

Nexel picked up Mack, that giant ignoramus putz and pain in the ass like nobody had ever been before, with only one hand, just like he was picking up a half-full grocery bag. Gone was the dramatic effort.

In the door, now he looked to Beverly and not Lem.

"Beverly, right? I'm leaving. Come along?"

"And start all over just with some new set of jerks? No thanks. This is the guy."

He shrugged, and then Nexel Five-Bone and Mack Azure were gone. They heard the car door slam, the car start up, the car drive off.

As the car drove off, Bev asked Lem, "How did you know who this guy was? Why didn't Mack kill you? He was certainly capable of it."

"Do you know what Mack told me in the car while you and Sophia were talking to that old couple in the RV, trying to get them to leave? He told me I was going to be his boss someday soon. I asked him why and he refused to say more, he even got out of the car instead of continuing the conversation. I believed him. That's why I knew he wouldn't hurt me."

"You knew for a fact?"

"I didn't know, but I *knew*."

"Okay," she nodded. "Watching you, I'm beginning to understand that you can know without knowing. You can decide to have no doubts while fully accepting that you do. Both of us are now officially crazy."

"Bev, you're growing. I told you. Welcome to adulthood. Now listen: I've got a plan," Lem said. "We have things to do. The plan will be ugly, disgusting, brutal, and awful. That's why I need you."

"I'm your girl," she put her arm around him. "Let's do it."

Bev felt empty inside.

Bev felt good.

24

Pot Of Gold

THE PLACE WAS DEAD from the outside-in. Bev was dead from the inside-out. They fit.

She'd lost something. She'd gained something. But like with Alzheimer's, when she went looking for what she was missing, it was gone, forever.

The sign out front said "École pour les petits fous." There were a couple of wooden signs on the lawn announcing "Now showing: Wit by Margaret Edson," but the dates were last month. The grass was dead from the hot summer sun. The parking lot was dead from the late Friday afternoon getaway. But there were buses running around back, and lights, and peeking through the windows on the way up. It was possible to see life, or at least signs of it.

She helped him out of the car, but he immediately smiled her off and struggled along towards the building. She wanted but couldn't carry his burden.

Inside the rooms they saw more lights, classrooms, and bright green decorations insisting they remember the upcoming Saint Patrick's Day. They got to the main doors. Somebody had propped one open with a rock. Inside, across the hallway, they could see a huge rainbow banner with the lettering "Reach For Me Pot O' Gold."

Bev opened the door. Cool, dry air and the stale smell of cafeteria cookies, cleaning supplies. Lemon.

"Lemuel, there's got to be a wheelchair around here, maybe a scooter. I could find a wheelbarrow in the gardener's shed. It'll only take a minute."

"Beverly," she thought he almost laughed, but that didn't make sense. "I can see you're trying. I can see that. But you need to stop hovering. If you're not around, and I don't do this for myself, who will help? Nobody. That's the point. I'm fine."

She saw his limbs shake. He saw her notice. She saw him stop them.

"You sure?"

"Yes. Trust me. Being a better person doesn't mean helicoptering over everybody. Let's move it."

By the door there was a clipboard roster of the students, probably to check them in and out of the metal detector. Lem looked at the security machines and shuddered, a leviathan surfacing in the distance, fat, dark clouds and a wet, bloody breeze blowing in over the thin waves.

He pushed off down the hall. She grabbed the list and trailed along, trying to help and not appear to be helping simultaneously. Stealth help. She found she was very bad at it. How could she be so helpful when she didn't feel it inside and so useless when she did?

"It's in the theater, here," he said a hundred feet and ten minutes later, reaching for the door.

The theater was locked.

They heard children's voices far away, laughing.

"Are there people here?" Bev didn't know what she would tell them. We're here for the tour?

"There's always people here in a school like this," he seemed happy in the memory, then he tugged again at the door. "Some things stay the same. Some things change over time. They always do."

"How much?" she wondered aloud, not expecting an answer.

He tried to peek through the theater door window but it was covered by something.

"I don't know. Maybe Tyler can tell us. We can find him. Sophie said the Scrambler was backstage."

He tugged again at the locked door. "If we can get in."

"They propped open the outside doors with a rock. Betcha they did it again," she said. "There's another entrance, it'll be around back."

She looked around. Getting Lem there was going to be another travail. She didn't want to say anything.

"Beverly," he said, "so we grab Tyler and this Scrambler. What then? What do you think? What would you do?"

She wasn't going to stay and chit-chat with Lem in the hall, and she wasn't going to leave him there. They began walking.

"I know a place," she said, listening to his breathing become more and more labored. "It's where I used to keep all of my, I guess you'd call them toys. If we can be invisible, and we can move around and fortify, if weapons work here like everything else works, we have a chance. I also think that we're so insignificant they might leave us alone."

That thought bothered her.

"Why have they left us alone so far?" He asked.

That thought bothered her more.

Finally they made it to the door labeled "backstage," and, as predicted, it was propped open like the other.

"Finally, some luck," she wanted to rush him in, to pick him up and carry him. Instead she waited patiently letting him go first. Thank God nobody came.

The dim auxiliary light made seeing difficult, so they both lumbered in further, explorers, wanting to swim into the scene and not just observe it. Beverly heard the door shut behind them. She checked it. Locked. She'd forgotten to put the rock back.

"Look for the emergency exits," she told Lem, rejoining him, "that's how we're leaving."

She'd never seen him look like this. Lemuel looked like a naked man in the freezing cold just being told his entire family died in the house fire in front of him. His mouth hung open. He looked at the sky, overcome by cold, unexpected fear.

He'd met a nightmare from his dreams, but there was nothing there, just junk.

That was strange. Was he having an episode?

Not knowing what else to do, she started looking around. It was supposed to be a box with lights.

The kids were in the middle of changing things up. Freshly cut sawdust. Construction paper. Scissors. Glue. A fake hospital bed, some folding chairs, and a desk were being moved offstage, a few boxes of green props taking their place. Saint Patrick had taken over and commandeered the children as slave labor towards the required ritual which was fast approaching.

She smelled cookies again. Peanut butter.

A bell rang. The kids were on to their next class, which might very well be here, she thought, moving quicker, nervously searching.

"Where'd she say the Scrambler was? If we can find a hiding place, I've got the roster from the front door, and we can work out getting your friend's child. Name's Tyler, right?"

Lemuel remained silent, frozen. Now she was getting worried.

"Lemuel."

"I lied."

"About knowing where the Scrambler is? Things change, I understand. You're right. Where do you think it might be? Should we move to another room? Is there a storage room, you know? ..."

"About everything," he interjected.

"We all exaggerate, take risks," she continued until his words registered.

All the air went out of her. After a bit, she took another ragged breath and continued.

"I don't understand."

Her words ran around on the ground and she wanted to stomp them before they got on her.

"About Tyler. About the Scrambler. About everything. All I knew was the school's name, and I only knew that because Mack told me."

She began checking the roster she was carrying. A hundred children, none of them named Tyler.

She started to say something several times. She looked at the roster again as if expecting Tyler to appear there. She heard kids outside in the hall. Nobody came in. It was late in the day. They might all be going home.

Mack lies. Mack always lies.

If the kids went home they couldn't snatch Tyler. Beverly's brain kept working a problem that she no longer had. She looked back to the roster. Nope, still not there. Looking to Lem, he had stopped staring at the sky and now looked at her with all of the sadness of the world in his eyes.

"I'm sorry, Beverly," was all he said.

Her mind spun.

"I don't understand. You lied about everything?" She thought if she repeated it back to him he'd realize he'd made a terrible mistake. He had to have meant something else.

"I believed."

"What?" Had she had a stroke?

There was a little smile. He looked down then back to her. He leaned, no he fell against one of the large crates. He remained standing, though. Somewhat.

"I felt if I could make it here," he said. "I had faith. I felt if I could make it here somehow."

With all of her being she willed this man in front of her to finish a sentence. To somehow fix whatever he was saying. There was too much.

"If we could make it here. I have faith," he said. "I felt it would work out. I believed."

She found that now that Lemuel was making sense, he was more insane than ever.

"Mark 16" he said.

"Sixteen what? Mark with a marker?"

She didn't have a marker.

"Let me tell you a story," he said as if that were the most natural thing in the world to say given their situation. "You'll like this."

She stared at him and nothing that could happen would surprise her more.

He continued. She was wrong.

"For almost two thousand years, ever since our earliest texts, we have known that the Gospel of Saint Mark ends with verse 8 of chapter 16. Sixteen hundred Greek manuscripts, and only three have something tacked on after that. Many of them have various other things added, but none of them agree. Had to have been added later."

He smiled more.

"It just ended with verse eight. But of course that wouldn't do. We couldn't have that. Do you know why?"

She slowly shook her head no.

"Because it ends with him dying. A first-hand account, probably our earliest account of all four Gospels, and he dies. You tried. You died. Too bad. So Sad. That's it. Do you find that troubling? Doesn't that bother you?"

She shook no again. She didn't care about any of it, but she didn't want to stop him. Maybe if he kept talking this episode would end. His tank of crazy would run dry.

"Used to bother me. Then I realized that for me it was probably the truest of all the gospels. It explained my life. I think it's how a religion can truly become universal. People lived under slavery, under oppression. The most powerful force ever known stepped on them and told them they were nothing. Somebody stepped forward and said no, they all mattered, they were all God's children. God loves them and there is hope. There is eternal life beyond this suffering."

His smile dimmed.

"Then they killed him, of course. We all know how it ends. Death. Impact. Meaning. It's the ultimate DIM story. No matter what text or complications they added after that, and they're still adding them, no matter what you feel about the rest of it, his faith, his life? Doesn't even matter if you're an atheist. That's not the point. It changed the world. Billions of people, people who don't even know or care about any of this, like you, lead better lives because of it."

"Lem, you're not making sense."

"Faith, Beverly. Hope without evidence. An inside connection to the outside of existence. Leaping into the unknown even if there's nothing there to leap to. That's what I thought I would do. That's why we're here."

He thought for a second, "We risk becoming a rerun. A good friend told me that once."

"What do you want us to do?" She thought that direct, simple questions might work.

"Break the pattern," he replied immediately.

Then he collapsed.

She immediately closed in on him, attended him on the ground. She knelt down and placed her hand on his shoulder.

"Let me help, please."

He was soaking wet in sweat.

He rocked a bit, "I'm okay. Thank you."

She didn't move back. She didn't remove her hand. Instead she worried.

He rocked again a couple of times. Then he stopped.

"But I can't walk," he said. He looked happy. He was happy he couldn't walk. Something had to have happened to her.

She let go, hit the ground in frustration and stood up.

"That's it, Lem," she said, looking around. "You're going to have to kill me. I'm already a Guardian, so I'll come back as a Guardian. Let me come back. I can help. We've never done that before. That's not a rerun."

She couldn't find anything, so she looked down at him. "I think. I believe, like you said. I'm with you, if that's what you want. And even if I don't come back? Maybe I just cycle and they'll leave you here. We win. I got you out. Let's do it."

He looked proud. That made no sense to her. Angry or sad would have worked.

"I can't, Beverly," he said. "I don't know how to kill people! I'm not the one to continue on, you are. I don't want to. And even if I did, which

I won't, I'm probably no good at it. I'd just screw it all up. How's that arm doing?"

She looked down at her arm in the sling.

"It hurts, but not that much," she tightened her lips.

She tested it.

"Wow. Actually, it's all better now."

He was smiling even more. She was realizing that she could not handle where this was going.

"Why don't you just shut the fuck up, Lemuel Rickenbacker."

"I want you to kill me," he said.

There. That was it. There they were. Here was the crazy place she never wanted to go again. She'd sworn that she'd never go there, but Lemuel had brought her here anyway.

"No," she worried.

"Do it or I'll do it myself," he said, "although I'm fairly certain it won't work like that."

"There's nothing," she said. She pleaded. "There's nothing here to hurt people with. It's a community center. What do you want? Glue you to the wall? Suffocate you with invisible tape? Wedgie you to death? I can do something, I can do it, but not like you want. It's not going to work."

He considered.

She continued, "And I don't want to. Lem, I'm just barely getting past all of that."

"Be creative," was all he said. Then he took the sharp edge of one of his crutches and started cutting into his own arm. He was demonstrating.

Keep up or die, Beverly, a small still voice told her. Keep up or watch him die.

"You're just going to do that yourself if I don't." It wasn't a question.

He ignored her, continuing to harm himself. She had to do something before he started doing real damage. He wasn't joking around.

He nodded yes. She shifted uncomfortably. She wanted to beat him. That would just help him. She was cornered.

Lem had taken her into the heart of the contradiction.

She replied before he got too far, "Do you realize the impact of what you're asking, both for me and you?"

He stopped. He nodded. But he did not look at her. He was waiting.

"Good," she said. "That's one of us. Ten minutes. Please Lem, I'm begging you."

As she went around gathering things, they continued to talk. The children's voices died off. The weekend was here. There was time. She had time. What else did she have?

He spoke up.

"I want you to tear me into little pieces, burn me with acid, torture me until I'm insane, and make my death as long and as painful as possible."

"I can't do that. I won't do that. I'm not that nice. You don't deserve it."

"You're the only person I've ever met that could do it right."

"I don't think I'm good enough. I'm not patient. You'll die too quickly."

She wanted to hurt herself like he did just to make him stop.

There, a laptop and a webcam. She set it up pointing to the middle of the stage. She could set up a delayed transmission. Some fiberglass that would make him itch for days.

"I'm almost dead already. You shouldn't have too much to do, but that might make it trickier. I didn't think about that. Can't be too quick."

He waggled his finger.

Ignoring him. There, a toaster. An old tire. She needed a gag, maybe some electrical cord.

A few more things needed. She stopped.

"Do you want me to write anything down? Tell anybody anything? I'll make sure the world sees it."

He shook his head no. She thought about pressuring him but changed her mind and went back to gathering, creating and constructing. Adjusting. Well Mack, here's my art. You finally get to see it, wherever you are. Your clay has become your statue. Lem will sing your sonnet. I composed it.

An old-fashioned electrical outlet timer. A toaster oven. There had to be a screwdriver, hammer, and some wooden dowels around here some-where. She needed a carving knife. The place reeked of recent woodwork.

"There, that's what I need," she announced.

Lem didn't say any more, he just watched with interest as she went about her work.

It wasn't ten minutes, but he didn't call her on it.

An hour later the building was completely quiet. She had finished.

"What have you made, Beverly? It looks quite creative."

She picked him up. She didn't ask. He was very light. She held him like a groom carrying his new bride across a threshold. She took him and began lifting him up to the tip of the post.

"This is going to hurt," she said.

"I hope so."

She got a gag out. She began putting it on but he stopped her.

"God loves you and no matter what you do, there is always a chance for heaven for all of us."

She completed the gag, silently, before he could say more. Shut up, Lem.

Lifting his body higher, she sat his anus on the pointy end of the large stick. She'd made it pointy, but not too pointy. She could feel the pain and thrashing. It was working.

She backed up to check her work. She owed him something. She didn't know what.

"Impalement would normally take several days and you would eventually bleed to death internally. I don't think that's enough for you. You deserve more."

It hurt. She hurt inside. She continued. He had faith. She would also have faith even if it was only in her own vile depravity.

"After a day or two, though, you'd be so delirious that you wouldn't really suffer that much," she gestured to other things. "That won't do. That's why the timer. Before you lose it, before you pass out, the timer kicks off the toaster oven, slowly igniting the tire. You'll die burning alive breathing in hot fire. You'll be insane by then from all of the itching."

She went to the exit door. She didn't want to finish telling him, but she did anyway.

"I've disabled the fire alarm. There's also a really good chance it'll ignite the building and take out the daycare above. Didn't notice the daycare when we came in, did you? Hopefully it'll be full of small children."

He didn't. He couldn't reply. His body was already thrashing. With each spasm the pole sank in a tiny bit more. He tried to still himself.

She opened the door. The bright sun blinded her.

"So there's a really good chance you'll kill a bunch of innocents as you die, hopefully making them suffer as well. I really hope so. It'll all be uploaded. The pain will multiply. They'll remember this a thousand years from now."

To nobody at all she said, "There you go, Mack. I got your fucking 'Ri' for your shuhari."

She started to leave but looked back one last time.

"It's all I could do, Lem. See you around. Thank you. I owe you my life. Right now I have a date with a wood chipper."

With the door closing and the bright sun almost blinding her, she said to nobody at all, "You lied. That's okay."

25

Good Day To Ride

HELL IS REPETITION, **H**ELL IS REPETITION. Bev thought as she finally came to. Hell is repetition. Was it really necessary, she thought, for hell to involve songs from the 1980s? Why did she have to remember? Why did they have to repeat?

She was back to where she started. It was Winkies, had to be. The thump-thump-thump of the old song brought her around and utter and sheer boredom of it all forced her to open her eyes even if she didn't want to. Dark, early morning maybe. She was sitting.

Thump-thump-thump, "Another One Rides The Bus." Then again.

Yup, that was Queen. A table. Again. The little placard said, "Nacho November! All nachos half price!"

Mother fucker. Looking up, the banner, "Welcome to Winkies!" and another one, "Disco Saturday Night! Dance Fever Karaoke!"

She wished she had a gun. Then the singing continued. She had to look. Two guns.

There was a karaoke screen.

Two young men, early twenties, stood side-by-side holding microphones. "And another one on, and another one on…"

May the devil save and keep her, that wasn't Queen. That was Weird Al Yankovic. Hell was far worse than she suspected. What would next time be? Dumbledore singing McArthur Park? The entire bar singing "Danny Boy"? Tony Bennett standards? My god, Nickelback? Would hell even go that far? Had they no shame? No limits?

She knew. She knew deep in her heart what would happen next. Mack was going to come back, and boy, was he going to be mad. Talk about making somebody look bad. Bev, in a life of making her own rules, had finally broken too many of them and had to pay.

"Where am I?"

She turned back to see a little boy, must have been seven or eight.

She smelled a burning tire.

She smiled at him, put on the loving grandma. "You're in a restaurant, dear. Nothing to worry about. Somebody will be along shortly to help you out."

"But there was a fire. My sister," he pleaded with her.

"Never you mind, sweet. I know for a fact she's fine. Just wait until you try the Nachos here. You like Nachos?"

He nodded.

"Then I'll order you some. When your nachos come, I'll show you a neat trick. Would you like to learn a trick?"

He nodded again. She saw a faint glimmer of hope.

"Good. You just wait. But you have to promise not to tell if I show you!"

A small smile. She had connected. He had a friend. Being nice came naturally. Connecting was always the first step in therapy. She used to preach that to her staff.

There was more she didn't tell her staff. Also why did being nice come naturally again like it used to? That wasn't right.

The boy reminded her of Lemuel. Somehow, though, he seemed even more broken than Lem was. Remembering them all, they all did.

Lem helped her. He connected with her, even if she didn't deserve it. Whatever happened, Lem was always there, pivoting, changing, moving with the flow. She would be bouncing off the walls. She, Beverly, the great fixer, in the end only amounted to a mundane little schemer. Lem was the real fixer. He would be just moving along, step-by-step.

He did not deserve what she did to him. Yet perhaps he did. She looked again at the boy.

She ordered him nachos. Before they arrived, however, a little girl walked in, walked up to the little boy, shook his hand, sat down, and instantly became his best friend.

She hadn't fixed the boy, but she provided a bridge, a Band-Aid. That would be enough.

Looking around, she realized that nobody had come for her. Who'd she have to screw to get service around here? She almost said it out loud, then smiled at the memory.

It was a sad smile. What if nobody came? Should she continue waiting or just go off on her own? Could she do that? Mack said when she was ready. Was that now? What more was left to do?

She started studying the entire bar, perhaps for the first time. At all the tables, people were seated in pairs. Made sense. Winkies was like that.

Except for Beverly. She was the only one sitting by herself. Alone again, naturally.

This was the real world, right? She could go her own way, wander off, find her new life. And why the hell not? As long as she stayed away from anything emotionally connected to her old life, Mack said it would be fine. Maybe she could set up her own grocery store.

He certainly wasn't here to stop her.

She could give it a spin again, only this time she knew a lot more about how the game worked.

"Is this seat taken?"

She turned her head. Lem!

She almost jumped out of her seat, but he pressed his hand on her shoulder and sat across from her.

"Oh my god, Lem! It worked! Did it work? If it worked, why are you here?"

He shushed her.

"Yes, it worked. We did what we needed to do."

Hitting the table, "Well?"

"Hmmm," he didn't seem eager to respond, as if working out how to do it.

She almost gasped looking at him. It was Lem and yet it was more.

He had no crutches or braces. That should have made him look half the size he used to look which wasn't that much to start with, but Lem had filled out. He had muscles. He still had the short haircut, the scar, and the acne scars, but he was firm, confident. Lem looked at peace. Gone was the turmoil she'd sensed every time he moved. He seemed content.

She suspected that he'd kept some of the bad parts of his appearance. Perhaps these parts pleased him. As if he had a choice in what he wanted to be or what he was going to look like.

Did he?

There was a word.

Fierce. Lem looked fierce.

"You look good, Lemuel," she said. "Now we can go back home. We can make a difference. Find Tyler."

A short shake no.

"I'm afraid I'm going to have to tell you some things. We're not going where you expected."

She almost laughed at him.

"What? Are you going to use profanity?"

"We…" he started, stopped, then started again, "our…Hmm. Reality has changed for us. You and I are going to need to change with it."

"You're telling me," she looked down. She didn't want to see him. "I see where this is going. I've done a lot of bad things. There's going to have to be payment, a balance. I treated you very badly. You wanted to do it personally. Somebody has to even things out. I understand. Go ahead. I'll take whatever's due me."

"No, no, gosh no, but I mean yes," he said. He seemed enormously pleased at his profanity and contradiction. "You don't deserve it, but I'm going to give this to you good and hard anyway."

"Go on, then. Don't make me wait. Going to take me out? Right here? Is there some lake of fire ants or a torture rack you need to find? Whatever. Give me the pain. You did it. I can too. I can take what I gave, at least try to."

"Pain? What pain? What are you talking about?"

"You're not here to hurt me?"

"Hurt you? Heavens no. I'm here to transform you."

"Cycling, right, the Buddhist thing? I have to work my way back up. Ok, I can do that. What am I going to be next time? A skunk? Head lice? Pond scum?"

"You just got promoted, Beverly Castler. No more DIM. We've done that. We're almost completely through the Guardian levels. Welcome to the MIT levels. Management-In-Training. I made sure."

She began crying. Beverly Castler hadn't cried since she was a teenager. He wasn't mad. There was a pain. The pain had to come forth, come out. It felt good coming out. Was she happy? It was awful. The pain made her happy.

He comforted her.

"I knew this would be difficult. I made it hurt as quickly as I could."

She smelled the sour breath of whisky first.

"Say? Who's up for a round of 'Sweet Caroline'? Don't you just LOVE that song?" The man was middle-aged, overweight, drunk, and leaning on their table. He was unsteady, leaning back and forth sailing on an ocean that only he could feel.

Beverly almost jerked back in fear. She was disgusted. She hated that song. Once started, it took days for it to stop bouncing on the music trampoline in her head. She tried to cover her reaction.

Without even looking at the man, Lemuel reached over and grabbed his forearm. The man made a squeak. He sounded like a mouse being slowly squeezed.

While she watched, the man reached his terminus, his end of the line. His arm grew older, more wrinkled. His skin became thinner. He lost weight, right while she was watching. His clothes were loose. His life disappeared. He looked like people on horror shows that have their souls sucked out of them.

The man became frail. He stooped. Finally he fell over and blew away as dust.

She looked around the room. Nobody seemed to take notice of him at all. There had to be a hundred people or more in the bar. The singing continued, the drinking continued. Somewhere somebody was having a fight on their cell phone. Two more people were walking to the stage.

"That was a mistake," Lem said, as if that explained everything. "He wasn't supposed to be here. At times mistakes happen. They've got to be corrected."

"This is your job now? You take people out? Why would you, of all people, want to do this?"

"It is the way. It is the path. Like you said, balance."

"Not my balance. Not your way either, as I remember. No thanks."

She crossed her arms, dared him. The hell if he was going to do that to her again.

"You sure? It's your chance, Bev. Isn't this exactly what you wanted when you first got here? You want to move ahead, we're moving ahead."

"What about all those things you've told me, the things you've tried to teach us all? Values? Morals? Character? Kindness?"

"Oh, that," he said as if he'd forgotten to get his keys on the way out the door and at the last minute saw them on the end table. "They're all true. And false. Depends on how you look at it. Balance. The utter chaos of total logic."

She let out a long, long breath.

"No," she said to him. "I'm not going back to that. I've learned. Enough, Lem. I'm not how I used to be. No matter what. I am here. You taught me. I learned. It was tough."

The little shit just ignored her.

"Beverly, we're going to go places beyond your wildest imagination and do things you never thought possible. Also," he continued, "You really should read your mail."

She patted her pocket. The letter was still there!

She tore it open. It had two handwritten parts.

The first part said, "Dear Ms. Castler, Our patient has been under treatment for three years. She continues to deny that anything happened as a result of your actions, even though at times she can accept the death. Unfortunately, she escaped two years ago and we haven't heard from her. Please, if she comes to visit you in prison, encourage her to come back. We love her and want to help her. She is very sick and needs treatment."

The bottom part, "They tell me that you killed my son, little Timothy Tyler. I want you to know that it is okay. I can never forgive you, but I am working hard on not carrying so much pain around inside.

Signed, Sophia Blackwell."

The letterhead showed that it was from the desk of "Director of Therapy, École Pour Les Petits Fous."

Horrified, she threw it down.

"No. Absolutely not. I'll just run off. You can't stop me."

"I'm sorry," he said. "I can stop you. You only leave here with me."

"Then demote me," she replied. "Take me back down. Make me a DIM level again. Mack said they could do that."

"See?" He said. "See what you're doing? Volunteering for pain? Asking for self-sacrifice? That's why I'm here. Selfless. You're not you anymore, yet you still are. You're ready."

He smiled at his own oblique self-reference.

"I don't get it, Lem. I'm trying to," she said, "You're happy that I'm acting like you? I can't be you. I never could be you. I'm a fake. I always have been. I'm not going to hurt anybody."

"Of course not," he said, "you still don't get it, nobody's asking you to do bad things. I've got that covered now. Aren't we friends? Would you be my friend?"

"Yes, yes, by all means yes. I have to say it?"

"Then our new reality will have some secrets, some tricks, some new powers. The only thing I'm not sure of is whether or not you are ready to really trust. That might be a jump for you. You're going to need that. We're in an organization now. Have you and I completed the work we began back at the taco stand? This is the choice I'm asking you…just this one choice: trust."

She couldn't help but notice that where his corncob pipe used to sit was a miniature golden sceptre. The gold had a dull blue glow.

"Others, no." She said, "not others. But I think I learned to trust now…I think."

"Beverly," he said again and held her hand.

"You, Lem," she said. "Trust you. I've learned to trust you even if you're wrong."

He took her other hand, gripped them both hard. He seemed pleased of his newfound strength. She didn't wither. She knew she wouldn't.

Looking from his hands to his eyes, she said, "I have faith. I don't know why. And I don't know what. But I have faith."

He winked at her. He had the warmest smile.

"Good. That's what we needed, the final piece. Our bus awaits."

"Bus?"

"Yeah, Bev, bus. Now we're bus drivers. Welcome to the first day of the rest of your life! Let's take a leap — together."

*"παντὸς μᾶλλον ἄρα, ἔφη, ὦ Κέβης, ψυχὴ
ἀθάνατον καὶ – ἀνώλεθρον, καὶ τῷ ὄντι ἔσονται
ἡμῶν αἱ ψυχαὶ ἐν Ἅιδου." Phaedo, 107a*

THE END

Afterword

There is no Winkies bar in Newark, New Jersey, at least as far as I know. I can most assuredly inform you that there is no Jim-Bob what that runs the Jim-Bob House of Corncobs.

The rest of it, I am not allowed to share -- at least not yet.